I0642649

HOT ROCKS

Stories of

Water and Desire

from the

South West Rocks Writers Group

Hot Rocks

All Rights Reserved

Copyright © 2017 is held by each of the individual authors.

Reproduction in any manner, in whole or in part,
in English or any other language, or otherwise,
without the written permission of the copyright holder is
prohibited.

This is a work of fiction and non-fiction.
Some names and identifying details have been changed to
protect the privacy of individuals.

For information address: mickiedaltonbooks@lycos.com

First Published in 2017

ISBN: 978-0-6480021-9-2

Editor: Robin Hammond
Artwork: Denise Delaney
Cover design: Michael Davies
Cover photograph supplied by Robin Hammond

Published by The Mickie Dalton Foundation
NSW
Australia

www.mickiedaltonfoundation.com

CONTENTS

Flash Fiction

Introduction

The South West Rocks Writers Group has been meeting and writing for approximately 21 years. The group originated under the auspices of Robyn Turner and meetings were at that time held weekly at the Pilot's Station. Members come and go, as with any such group, but some of us have been here since its inception. We now meet fortnightly for three-and-a-half hours of writing in the South West Rocks Nursing Home conference room.

So far, we have refused to bow to the convention of having a formal committee structure, our writers taking turns to lead the group in writing exercises which are stimulating, fun and always challenging. It takes a fair amount of courage to read one's work out in public and then submit to a group critique but our fellow writers provide a safe, unjudgemental and open-minded space in which to do this.

SWRWG consists of published and aspiring authors and those who just enjoy writing. We range in age from early thirties to, well, really quite old. In this anthology, you will find stories and poetry from many genres: fantasy, memoir, non-fiction, science fiction and just plain fiction. There is romance, passion, violence, sadness, laughter – and some very strange happenings. The stories and poems are influenced by the overarching themes of water and/or desire.

Hot Rocks is the second anthology produced by our group, the first being *Tales from the Rocks* (2012). The publication of this anthology was suggested by Desley Polmear, a former long-standing member of our group. We would like to thank the many people involved in its production. Our special thanks go to the SWR Nursing Home, which allows us the use of its conference room for our fortnightly meetings.

We trust you will enjoy dipping into the pages of this, our second anthology.

SHORT STORIES,
POETRY
AND
'POSTCARDS'

A collection of tales from our inventive writers. The only rule: length up to approximately 2,000 words. Mostly fiction, some are non-fiction, others are autobiographical. Our stories are interspersed with poetry and the occasional 'postcard' with a twist.

Hot Rocks

Oh No, Not Me

Denise Delaney

The oval orifice oozes O ... Onomatopoeia.

O obeys and digs its feet in the ground.

It puts the OM in omniscient and hides its head in the sand.

O is ornate, ormolu, opulent and overblown.

O offends, obsesses, occludes and oppresses. An odalesque observing the naked rule is deemed obscene by the oily, odious and officious, who ogle, who leer, then order overcoats.

O made me omnivorous and it made me obese.

Oh ... orange dust tickles my olfactory organ, and I expel an orgasmic sneeze, and I am, 'Oh god, oh god, oh god, oh god' for a few seconds omnipotent. 'Ohhhhh'

'Oh, more please God, okay?'

Oh no, not, nay, no bloody way,

No such luck, nick off, go away,

Go jump in the lake, this I deny,

I refuse, I rescind, I nullify,

Shove it, nix, it's all for nought,

Nothing doing, revoke, I baulk,

Zero, zilch, not happening today.

Oh ... I'll think about it. Okay?

I rub my face in orange blossoms, throw pepper in the air, breathe deep to no avail, then try to tickle with my hair.

A sneeze, perfect, profound, a precious little dance between me, myself, alone and the elusive God of Chance.

In the great gambling den in the sky, a god grins, a game begins, a bottle turns, a marble bounces, a die rolls, a penny spins, a handle is pulled, pictures rotate and a child says 'eeny meeny miney moe'. I hold my breath. I hope. Oh yes. Oh no. It's me. Oh, not so.

The god smiles at my libido.

A number drops down, and glows, then strobes, and a feather materialises under my nose.

I send thanks and a silent ovation, then relax for the little deaths, oblivion, exultation.

Sophie

Robin Hammond

On a bench beneath one of the big fig trees, she waited patiently for me. As I approached, I could see Paula had nestled a little pink bow in her curls – so cute – and she was watching with big eyes a group of her little friends playing with a ball on the grassy slopes of the park. She was so good, the way she sat there, obedient to Paula's instructions, until she saw me and, with an excited cry, slipped off the bench and ran into my open arms. Sophie, my sweet girl! I held her warm, squirming body to my chest while, over her head, I watched Paula's car pull out from the kerb and drive away, a hand waving from the driver's window. As Sophie scrambled down and I pushed her gently in the direction of her little friends, I glanced at my watch. Two hours of unsupervised access – not much, but at least it was something.

When it first happened and I'd been forced out of my home, Paula had broken off all contact between me and Sophie for several months. Sure, I had screwed up big-time but I thought her reaction was over the top. I'd been drinking a bit too much, I suppose, but thought I was handling it pretty well. Work at the call centre was getting to me: all those unresponsive, curt or downright rude people on the other end of the line. And the long hours for minimum wages – you know how it is. Well, the self-medication might have got a bit out of hand, I guess, but as I say, it was only when I began tossing back a vodka or two with breakfast, just to set me up for the day, that things became serious.

First, one Saturday afternoon, I forgot to pick up Sophie from a play-date with her little friend, Rex. Paula was furious when she came home from working a late shift at the supermarket to find a neighbour's note saying Sophie had been left with her. Her repeated knocking had been unable to rouse me from the nap I'd taken after lunch. I admit the 'nap' did extend into early evening and the neighbours were pretty pissed-off by the time Paula got around to collecting Sophie.

The next thing that happened was I lost my job. Apparently, clients had complained about my rudeness but really, if you only knew how rude they were to me... Anyway, I figured being a house-husband would be right up my alley *and* I'd have lots more time with Sophie. She was almost a year old by then and a real daddy's girl. At first, it went well: we took walks together, we played with the ball in the park, on hot days we ran around under the sprinkler, shrieking and yelping with delight.

Then, one day, when Paula came home, she couldn't wake up Sophie from her afternoon nap. Well, it *was* 9 p.m. and Sophie and I had crawled under the covers together and crashed out around 4 o'clock. In fact, I myself was sleeping so soundly it took a fair bit of tugging and screaming on Paula's part to wake me, too. I mumbled something about her taking Sophie to the doctor but Paula rushed into the laundry with her and dunked her in a tub of lukewarm water, whereupon Sophie gradually came to, her eyes rolling a little, but perfectly fine, really. Paula swore she could smell alcohol on Sophie's breath but I denied that absolutely. I mean, why would I do that?

So I was given a final warning. That's exactly how she put it: 'This is your final warning, Jason!' And she laid down all these strictures: the house was getting too messy; from now on Sophie was only allowed to play outside. I mean, really! How much notice was I going to take of that? Sophie was getting too fat, presumably because I was feeding her too much junk food: set meal times, lean meat only, no fat, blah, blah, blah. And discipline was becoming another thorny issue. In my view, Paula was far too strict and I took great delight in breaking all the rules she set down for curbing Sophie's more rambunctious behaviours. Paula didn't want Sophie in our bed, for instance. 'She's got a perfectly comfortable bed of her own, Jason,' she'd say, sweeping out of the bedroom with Sophie who peered beseechingly back at me with those big brown eyes. If only she was able to talk; I was sure she'd be pleading for 'Daddy!'

That was just before the final bust-up. Sitting on the bench I watched Sophie who, by now, had moved with her little friends to splash in the shallows of the park lake. We hadn't had rain for a while and the water level was dropping so there was a fair bit of mud around the edges. Sophie was getting pretty dirty but I was reluctant to drag her away from all that fun. I would have to find a tap before Paula returned, though. It was mud that caused the last big catastrophe which saw me hunted out of my home.

This is how it happened. Obeying Paula's instructions (for once), I'd sent Sophie outside into the backyard to play, while I spent some quality time with my games console and a glass or three of vino. An hour or so later, when I remembered to check on her, I found her playing in the compost heap amongst the old vegetable peelings, rotting food scraps and chook manure. She was in a right state: filthy, smelly and covered in mud, from where she'd tipped over the drinking water in the chookyard.

'Sophie!' I cried, 'Naughty!' I seized her and bore her inside, checking my watch to make sure I had enough time to get her cleaned up before Paula arrived home from work. We had a good two hours, so I figured I could do it. I wrapped Sophie in a towel and ran a shallow, lukewarm tub with plenty of bubbles and a good dollop of Paula's best bath essence then plopped her in and began scrubbing and shampooing. She wriggled with delight, splashing and rolling around in the water, loving every minute. What the heck – it looked like fun, so I stripped off and climbed in with her, not forgetting the rest of the wine I'd been swigging while she played outside.

The next thing I recall was a loud shriek of absolute horror. I dragged myself out of the depths of the sleep into which I'd fallen, to find Paula standing thunderstruck in the bathroom. 'What the fuck do you think you're doing!?' she screamed.

I looked around, blearily. Yeah, the room was a bit of a mess: there was mud all over the towels and muddy puddles on the floor, splashes of dirt across the walls. Sophie was okay but she was sitting at the end of the bath shivering and looking pretty miserable. And she was whimpering a bit, I suppose.

Well, I needn't go into all the sordid details except to say that Paula did that undignified thing that you see the aggrieved parties (usually women) do in movies: she threw all my stuff out onto the front lawn – clothes, games console, tablet, shoes, laptop, all my old stuffed toys, everything. Then she shoved me out the door and locked it. This was after telling me that in no circumstances would I ever see her or Sophie again. The neighbours witnessed everything and it was all pretty embarrassing.

After that episode, I worked on mending my ways and gradually Paula relented a little. She allowed me supervised visits with Sophie and, after my constant pleading, we got to the stage of this experimental two-hour period of unsupervised access at the park. So you can see why I was pretty anxious to get Sophie cleaned up before Paula came back to collect her.

Fortunately, I found a tap and got some paper towels from the kiosk and cleaned Sophie's feet as best I could. Then we sat down on the grass and polished off an ice cream each. As a special treat, I bought a large block of dark chocolate and before I'd realised it, Sophie had eaten almost the entire block and was happily licking over the chocolate wrapper.

It was then a shadow loomed and I heard a familiar sound, that of Paula's indrawn breath followed by: 'What the hell is going on here!?' I must admit a shadow of apprehension swept over me when I saw Paula's face but I couldn't for the life of me understand why she looked so pale and shocked.

'We're eating ice cream and chocolate,' I explained. 'Look, Sophie ate a whole big block, all by herself, greedy little thing.' I was rather proud, actually. Sophie looked up at Paula and smiled, licking chocolate from her lips. Before I could move, Paula had swept Sophie up and was running with her towards her car. I scrambled to my feet and followed. 'Paula, stop!' I cried, 'what are you doing?' Paula did not answer; she had Sophie in the backseat and was fumbling with her harness. I grabbed Paula's shoulder and tried to turn her to face me but she shrugged me off. 'Paula, listen. I just want to know, when can I see Sophie again?'

Paula stood still for a moment. Then she turned and looked me in the eye with that basilisk glare she did so well. As usual, I quailed. 'Jason,' she said, 'do I have to remind you that Sophie is a dog? You do not give alcohol to dogs, you do not wash with them in the bathtub, or sleep with them in the matrimonial bed. You do not feed them fast food and especially, you do not allow them to eat large quantities of chocolate that will put them in danger of serious illness or even death. Now, I am taking Sophie straight to the vet and you will have to hope for your sake that she's all right. The only contact you'll have from me in future is the vet's bill that I'll drop into your mailbox. Other than that, you'll never see or hear from me or Sophie again. Is that clear?'

I could only nod dumbly as she climbed into her car and sped off down the road. I turned and headed for home. How come Paula knew so much about this sort of thing? I never knew chocolate was bad for dogs. I'd have to go home and google it. Long, empty months stretched ahead. Miserable, I sighed and turned left, heading for the bottle shop. A bit of restorative self-medication would seem to be in order, once again.

Postcard from Pitcairn Island

Craig Slobin

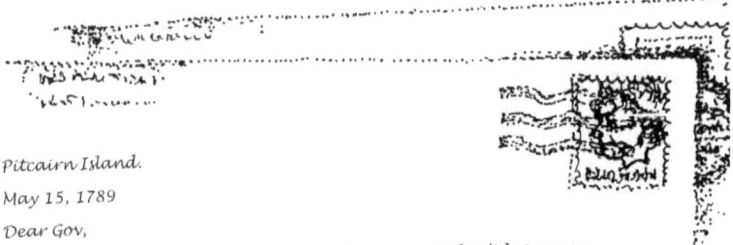

Pitcairn Island.

May 15, 1789

Dear Gov,

I hope you made it home. I hope the currents don't bring you back. Now, I know what you're going to say, but you're wrong. Just because these women aren't Christians doesn't make them less of a people. Besides, with a surname such as mine I'm sure our forgiving God will look kindly on them, and us. It hasn't rained once since we've been here, nothing but pristine sands, crystal clear waters and glorious sunshine. Surely if Jesus was upset we'd be soaking wet, cold to the bone and starving to death. Maybe our righteous God is actually angry at you, not to mention every other bastard back in the Old Country. After all, he rains every day on you lot.

Anyway, this is simply a courtesy postcard hoping you are well thanking you for your ship. I hope Her Majesty isn't too upset with you, especially when you tell her we sank the Bounty to the bottom of the ocean.

Yours sincerely, and rather happily,

Fletcher Christian

Emily's Secret

Desley Polmear

In the steaming heat, Emily Forsythe took great lengths to prepare the food for the christening lunch. She wondered if she'd recognise Jane and Antonio after all these years. They'd been living in Italy for the last ten years and the only communication between the two women was an occasional email, perhaps near Christmas. She saw the white Jaguar arrive in the circular drive, followed by Sam and Penny's white Holden in the distance.

Jane strutted into the room wearing a long, flowing creation in aqua and pink with matching flat shoes. 'Hello darling, here's the champagne. Let's pop the cork and relax?' Antonio carried a small Esky in one hand and a stuffed bag in the other. The moment Emily saw Antonio, time stopped briefly. They both locked eyes and swapped a lingering smile. She looked away first.

After the greetings, Emily spoke to her husband Daniel, quietly. 'Can you take the guests out onto the patio? I've still got the finishing touches to do here.'

'Of course babe!'

When Emily finally appeared, the guests were being amused by Daniel. His Pommy jokes were flowing. God, how many times had she heard them? He liked to take the floor but they were always the same old jokes. She placed a tray of snacks and an ice bucket on the wooden setting they were here to christen. It was Daniel's first attempt at woodwork since attending the men's shed.

'Please, help yourselves?' She waved her hands toward the food. 'This is what we are here to christen. This is Daniel's handiwork, the finished table.'

'Crap,' said Antonio. 'When have you become a handyman?'

'Well I can vouch for his excellent work,' Emily said, raising her glass. 'Definitely his work from start to finish, cross my heart.'

Over lunch, Antonio and Jane were full of it, bragging about their lavish lifestyle since their company came onto the share market, and the private holistic boarding school in the country their two children attended. She wondered what her close friends Penny and Sam thought.

'How old are Josh and Polly now?' asked Antonio.

'Josh is turning seven this year and Polly almost five. You would have met them except my sister Cassie took them to the circus and a sleepover.

'Where do the years go? Our eldest, Mark, is nearly nine and the twins are seven. Oh, and by the way, how does it feel to be turning forty this year Danny boy?'

'You're not far behind me.'

Antonio raised his glass, chuckling. 'True. The years we spent in Italy seemed to fly. Of course the kids were against coming home. Anyway they've finally settled back now and

Mark and the twins love the boarding school. It's mainly guided towards gifted children.'

Emily took a deep breath, and stopped herself. Her own two children were doing quite well in the public system. 'Just as well you have the money as I believe it's quite expensive there.'

'Hey, since we're talking about money,' interrupted Daniel. 'When do you think those bloody investments are going to make some money? We're still struggling today thanks to your wise investment plan.' He smirked before taking a swig of his beer.

'This is not the time,' Emily said, giving him a kick under the table. 'Anyone want dessert?' She began to clear the table, the other women helping to carry the empty plates into the kitchen.

'Penny, could you fetch another bottle from the bar fridge on your way out please?' She shooed them back outside, hands full, and stood, eyes closed, thinking about that investment. They'd put all their confidence in Antonio. It was a sure thing, he'd said. Still, they'd learnt over the years it wasn't entirely his fault. They had made the final decision. She checked her blouse in the small mirror for food stains, before grabbing the rest of the eats, sauntering out to the guests with a fruit and cheese platter in one hand, a lemon cheesecake and a small tub of ice cream in the other.

After dessert, they retired to the patio on the cooler side of the house near the pool. Emily lounged back into the sofa fondling her pendant. 'What are you staring at?' she said quietly to Antonio.

'The pendant.' He leant in closer, whispering. 'You've kept it all these years.'

***

'Okay now everyone's changed into their bathers, who's ready to jump in? And who's up for a game of water polo?' said Daniel.

'I'm in,' said Sam.

'Sounds like fun. Just a moment – Antonio, another wine,' said Jane, her voice slurring slightly. She indicated her empty glass, hand shaking, then walked to the edge of the pool and stood, balancing herself preparing to dive.

'I'll get the wine,' said Emily. She wandered into the kitchen but she could feel Antonio's presence as she opened the refrigerator door.

'I've missed your company all these years Em.'

'Don't, Antonio. That was so long ago and I'm now a happily married woman. Daniel's a good man. We've struggled along together and stood by each other. That bad investment you led us to left a sour taste in our mouths and it caused a lot of heartache between us.'

'I felt bad too, at the time. Remember though, it was entirely your decision.' He paused. Eyes locked with hers he took a step closer. 'I lost money too. Things like that happen during a lifetime but you can't beat yourself up about it the rest of your days. I struggled through that bad period. But then, through luck and hard work, things came good eventually.'

'You're right. I know you've done well, but for us it's been difficult. We had to start from scratch almost. We were lucky that Daniel's Dad helped us out financially.'

He put his hand out, but she moved away. 'Em, please? What about your feelings for me? Did you ever think of me after I went overseas? You loved me to the moon and back once.'

'You're right, I did. But who did the cheating? Jane was my best friend, remember. You're lucky I'm still speaking to you both.'

'I know. I think of it often. The truth is, Em, I chose the wrong girl. It's been ten long years climbing the ladder, and my company has taken me to lots of great places. Places I wished you were with me, instead of Jane.' He touched her arm but she took a step back. 'Look, I'm in town for the next seven days or so before I head off for a few weeks in Switzerland. Could we meet up and have lunch together? It'd be just like old times. There's so much I'd like to talk to you about.'

'That's definitely out of the question.' She grabbed the plastic tray, clean glasses, and bottle of wine and went back onto the patio, her body shaking. Everyone was in the pool, hitting the ball back and forth, laughter filling the air. She raised the bottle to Jane before placing it in the ice bucket. She moved back into the house to grab her sarong; she would join them in the pool. Antonio was there, leaning against the kitchen bench, arms folded. His eyes fixed on hers.

'I want to touch you Em. Come to me?' Something in her wanted touch, his touch. It'd been so long. 'Please, just let me hold you.'

'We both know it's not right Antonio,' she said, motionless. He opened his arms, beckoning. He'd always had a knack of recognising instantly whether he had a good chance or not with women.

Emily seemed to be hypnotised as she stared into his piercing brown eyes. A sharp jolt of need hit her deep in her gut. Memories flooded back of the love and closeness they once had for each other. She was the lucky one back then as every girl in town wanted Antonio Sebastian Verde, the handsome Italian.

'Em, come to me?'

His voice was husky, sexy, like she remembered when he'd made love to her. She took small steps towards him, not once dropping her eyes. Her head fell onto his chest, arms by her side. His strong arms wrapped around her, pulling her closer. Besides his beating heart, the ticking grandfather clock from the hallway was the only other sound in the room. She felt safe in his arms, like she used to. She was hit with an instant flashback to 1989 as she breathed in the familiar scent of his aftershave. He took her hand. Electricity ran through her body like a lightning strike, her pulse racing as she laced her fingers through his, hands interlocking. He leant down and met her parting lips. She waited for the thrust of his tongue. She didn't pull away, she didn't want to. As he bent to kiss her flesh, her breathing quickened. She knew without a doubt that what was happening to her was not right morally, but in this moment, she wanted him.

He led her with urgency to the adjoining room and turned the key. The outside sounds were drowned out by the sound of his heavy breathing. He ground his hips against hers, moaning with excitement, his breathing quickening, his panting louder.

'I've never stopped loving you, Em.' Breathless, he struggled to remove her bikini.

Emily closed her eyes and went to another time – a time before Jane.

***

'Oh Em, we both needed that.' His head fell into the crook of her neck. 'You're full of surprises.'

Emily fixed her clothing. 'Please Antonio can you busy yourself in the kitchen?' Antonio ran the hot water and began washing the dishes.

Daniel watched as Emily walked towards the pool in her bikini, towel draped over her shoulder. He grinned as she dived into the pool towards him. He embraced her when she bobbed back up. 'I've missed you. We had a cracker of a game. The men won hands down. What've you been doing all this time?'

'Antonio was helping me in the kitchen. You know how I like it tidy straight away.' He nodded, kissing her on the cheek. They both went under the water, doing handstands and kissing on the way up like they always did. When she surfaced, she shot a quick glance at Antonio, who had entered the pool. His back was against the pool wall, his olive skin glistening. She dived under the water once more, not wanting to see his scowl and his thin, straight mouth. Thoughts raced through her head. Thoughts riddled with guilt. She clung tightly to the one who truly loved her, the one who fell asleep in front of the TV each night, the one who spooned into her each evening in the matrimonial bed.

***

'Well old boy, it's after 9 o'clock. It's about time we headed off. It's been good catching up again. To think you made that table still shocks me,' Antonio said. 'Perhaps when we get back from Switzerland we'll get together again. What do you reckon?'

'Sure anytime.'

Emily stood, noticing the single shaft of moonlight illuminating the brass doorknob. 'Well our life is quite busy the rest of the year,' she said. 'I have family visiting from overseas and lots of things will be happening. I doubt we'll have time. Goodbye Antonio, Jane.' She reached up and pecked them on the cheek.

After waving the visitors goodbye, Emily walked inside, pleased. Antonio hadn't changed. He was a born user and womaniser. The moment of pleasure with him was gone, gone forever. Her thoughts lay with her husband, steady authentic and loving Daniel. He was someone she could trust and love for the rest of her days.

Under the Sea

Craig Slobin

Usually, Desiree would find Malcolm's singing funny but she was in a foul mood; besides, she hated Disney.

'Under the sea, under the sea, under the ... SEA!' the song belted into her earpiece.

'Very funny, Mal,' she said into the microphone on the console. 'Hilarious, just as hilarious as yesterday when you sang that damned song, and the day before that, and the damned day before that.'

'Sourpuss,' was the reply in her ear, 'sheesh, who doesn't like, *The Little Mermaid*?'

'Me, that's who. Now, did you see any sign of them?' She looked out the observation window, her petulance turning to worry at what she saw. He was alone out there. They had been missing for two hours now. Usually she wouldn't be so anxious. All of them got side-tracked down here at the bottom of the Pacific, the bottom of the world. James and Terrance, however, only had half-an-hour of oxygen left in their tanks. When that time ran out, well, their lives would run out with it.

She was a good team leader and did everything by the book. That was why Malcolm had been sent out when the other two were only one minute late. She wished everybody else would follow the book as well. Unfortunately for her, the rest of the team were lax. These ridiculous headsets only had a distance of three kilometres, too; anything could have happened to them.

'Nope,' said Malcolm with a chuckle.

'Shit!' she cursed. 'Well, well ... shit!' She spun her chair around and pushed off so she rolled over the observatory's grilled floor and butted into the desk with the computer which held the emergency protocols in it. 'Shit! Shit! Shit!' she spat, as she hurriedly clicked on the missing crew member icon and typed in how much air they had left.

Yet, just as she began reading, Malcolm's chuckles turned to laughter. At first, his antics shocked her before her shoulders slumped in relief and she launched herself back to the window to stare out at him floating outside in the gentle currents.

'Very funny, Mal,' she said with a smirk. This time she meant it. 'Where are they?'

'Where do you think they are, my sensational siren?' he replied. She could even see his smiling eyes behind his mask, he was so close. Despite her obvious relief she was still a tad frightened for James and Terrance, one a current boyfriend and one an old one.

'C'mon, Mal,' she pleaded. 'No more games.'

'Fine, my illustrious leader,' he sulked. 'They're in the ravine chamber. They didn't have enough air to make it back to base.'

'Thank god,' she muttered. In truth, she didn't know which one she was more worried about. She wished the benefactor, Mr Samuel, had run the names of the members of this expedition by her before signing them up. Of the six divers down here aside from herself, she was, or had been, romantically involved with four of them. She supposed it was only natural. After all, Mr Samuel wanted only the best divers in the world and so did she. He, for his project down here, and she because she found other men, well, boring. So it was bound to happen eventually. Sooner or later she was destined to have to work with an ex-boyfriend or her ex-husband. She never expected to have to work with all of them – not all at once. James, her boyfriend, Terrance, her ex-boyfriend, David, her ex-husband, and even George, a one-night stand after a conference; okay, five one-night stands, those conferences *were* incredibly boring. The only two she hadn't slept with were her old instructor and mentor, Malcolm; and Dr Billie, of course. In actual fact, she had always wanted to bang Malcolm, but that was twenty years ago at college; now he was a wrinkly old man, and Billie, well, Billie was female and she didn't roll that way.

James had told her that Billie certainly did. She probably could sleep with the attractive, big-breasted doctor if she really wanted too. George said that Billie had a crush on her as big as a whale.

Maybe I should, I'm sick of men.

She knew that was a lie. She was just sick of being surrounded by the wrong men, all of her bloody exes.

'No, thank me, my little mermaid,' returned Malcolm with another chuckle as a cloud of bubbles surrounded his head. 'Anyway, my flirtatious female, your beau, and your old beau, are waiting for me to bring new tanks to them. If they don't kill each other first,' he added, with a glint in his eye.

She arched a brow at him, 'Very funny.'

'So you keep saying, my beautiful boss,' he chortled.

'Well, get into the decom chamber and I'll have David meet you there with the oxygen tanks. You can both go,' she instructed. David was a stuck-up prick, but he was dependable and solid. Besides, it would make him feel better having to save her current boyfriend's life; make him feel better than James. For the past week he had been moping about down here every day and it was driving her bonkers. After all, they'd divorced over five years ago.

'Your wish is my command, my fantastic floozy.' Malcolm nodded before diving down and out of sight. She caught herself just before she said, 'very funny,' again.

With a quick tap on the overhead button she had access to every room in the base, or her voice did. 'David, we found them,' she said into the microphone. 'They're out at the ravine chamber. Can you meet Mal in the decom and help him take some tanks to them ... please?'

Hot Rocks

It was always best to be polite with David. He enjoyed people grovelling to him, it made him feel important. For the next ten minutes she simply sat looking out at the ocean floor. Night was approaching up above on the surface and with its arrival the dim light down here was disappearing fast. Finally, she saw what she was waiting for: two light beams from their torches, Malcolm and David.

'Good luck, fellas,' she wished them well. 'And be safe.'

Eventually the twin lights vanished into the depths as they descended into the ravine and she was alone again. She didn't like night at the bottom of the ocean, even on a good day, and this wasn't a good day. She waited there so long she almost dozed off.

'Hey, gorgeous,' greeted a female voice. Desiree gave a tiny start at the sudden noise behind her, which caused the beautiful doctor to smile at her, with deep dimples. 'Bit jumpy, aren't we?' grinned Billie. 'You know what you need? A massage!'

Usually she would have refused the angelic lesbian but damn her if she didn't need somebody's touch right now. She even groaned in delight when Billie's long hands began soothing her tight shoulders. It was a wonderful massage ... until she felt the doctor's lips caress her earlobe. Thankfully, she didn't have to remonstrate with the woman for George walked in.

'Well, well,' he grinned as Billie jerked back from Desiree's ear, 'hellloo, laadiiees.' The idiot even rubbed his hands together. 'Care for another body?'

'Schmuck,' said Billie with a smirk, but before she could resume her massaging, Desiree used her legs to roll the chair back over to the emergency computer, thus avoiding any further confusion; for Billie or herself, she couldn't say.

'Hey,' she said as she frowned at the time on the bottom corner of the screen. Maybe she *had* fallen asleep. 'How long have Mal and David been gone?' She wasn't really asking, she knew how long, the time was right there in front of her. 'Shit!'

'How long?' asked George, with concern finally breaking through his ambitions of a threesome. Knowing him, it probably wouldn't be his first, he was definitely the most skilled in bed of her exes. And her current one, truth be told.

'Too long,' she replied anxiously. 'The ravine chamber's one hour away and they've been three.'

Billie sighed, making certain her breasts almost popped out of her skimpy top with no bra on. 'C'mon, Georgie boy,' she said as she slapped his shoulder, 'looks like we're up.'

'Shit,' he replied, as he deflated, all wishful desires leaving him, until Billie's next words.

Hot Rocks

'I'll lead the way and you can perve on my tight arse for two hours,' she offered with a cheeky slap on his, and a wink for Desiree. So she was left alone again, for a very long time too. So long, in fact, that she did fall asleep. Her dreams were consumed with dreadful images of her friends drowning out there in the cold blackness. When she did wake, her eyes were blurry and full of sleep but a familiar sound kick-started her brain. The stupid song made her leap out of the chair and press her face up against the thick glass of the observatory in joyful relief.

'Under the sea, under the sea, under the ... SEA!' There they were, it was dark; pitch black, in fact, but she counted six torches in a long line returning to base.

'Woohoo!' she yelled into the microphone. 'Well done, Mal! Well done! I'm so happy I'll even let you make me watch *The Little Mermaid* with you tonight!'

'Oh, my mesmerising mermaid, we were going to watch it anyway,' he chuckled in reply. 'All of your problems are over.'

She grinned. All of her problems were over, everyone was safe and back. She knew she should've stayed in the observatory but she was simply too happy. She ripped the earpiece out and raced off to the decom chamber getting there just in time to see the first diver climb out of the dark water.

Elated, she wrapped Malcolm up in a fierce bear hug. She didn't even mind his cold and dripping wetsuit. She wasn't sure exactly when her glee was replaced by confusion; maybe when she saw the long rope tied to him with five torches attached every six metres. Terror struck when Malcolm pushed his saggy, purple lips against her own and whispered in her ear before kissing that too.

'Finally, my hard-to-get harlot,' he said soothingly. 'Finally, it's just us down here, my little mermaid.' Her very soul went as cold as ice as he began to sing in her ear, while his wrinkly hands caressed her breasts:' Under the sea, under the sea, under the ... SEA!'

Morning Winch-up
(on prawn trawlers)

Diane Jensen

Last shot for the night, bags emptied onto tray,
Nets streaming in the ocean, washing clean.
Winches silenced, bodies tired.

A red ball is sifting rays
through grey awakening clouds;
rising
Slowly changing into molten yellow;
Laying down its golden carpet
Across a raven sea.

Follow this path of gold
Though it might blind you,
toward the heart of fiery treasure;
Reach, before it climbs into heaven
to dominate again, another day –
while we sleep.

Lizard People

Stella Perkins

'What do you mean? They are already here.'

I was listening to a conversation in a coffee shop, the way you do when you sit alone sipping at your cappuccino. The conversation was taking place at an adjoining table between two men, both dark and looking to be in their early forties. I pretended to be engrossed in a magazine while I sipped my coffee, spooning up scoops of froth and chocolate and smelling the rich aroma of the fresh pastries. This was the way to gather material for novels. This was the way to absorb atmosphere and conversation. Outside in the street, a sudden downpour of rain made people scatter for cover; some took shelter in the shop. The two men paused in their conversation and watched the newcomers warily. The storm was short-lived. The sun came out leaving the pavements steamy and smelling of damp earth and summer storms. The conversation resumed.

'How do you know they have been here for a generation?' asked the indignant shorter man.

'Keep your voice down. This is highly classified information. I shouldn't even be talking about it.' No, I thought; let alone talking about it in a crowded coffee shop in the heart of Newtown.

'Look, you've seen them heaps of times. Why you even nick-named one Sleazy Lizard.'

'You can't mean boring old Nick Robinson. There is nothing alien about him. Why he is the most ineffective, inefficient, inept example of a human being.'

'Exactly.' His companion nodded. 'You know how Nick likes to sit there nodding wisely with that stupid grin on his dial, just like a lizard, looking as though he is listening to every word you are saying, but all the time, deep down in your boots you know his mind is thousands of kilometres away... you know how he likes to rest his elbows on the table with his fingers laced together under his chin? What he is actually doing is...'

The waiter moved in front of me and clanged the cups and saucers he was collecting and I missed the next part of the conversation. I stood and moved past their table, trying to catch the rest of what they were saying.

Who were the lizard people?

I thought of the number of professionals that I knew, my own bloody doctor for one, who does that sage lizard smile, that sleepy nod, that prayer-like formation of the fingers to form a what? Why the steepling of the fingers? I had to find out.

Slipping out of my coat, so they would not be looking for a beautiful woman in a smart red jacket, I began to follow them. They moved along the street peering in shop windows. Presently, they stopped in front of an antiques shop. I saw them glance at the man behind the counter, nudge each other and move towards the door. I sidled up to the shop window and peeped inside. The man behind the counter was reading a newspaper spread out before him, with his elbows resting on the counter and his fingers steepled under his chin. I watched as the two men approached the counter. The man behind the counter had a widow's peak in his dark hair, his thin face was thrust forward and he had a receding chin line. A more lizard-looking man you would be hard-pressed to find.

So these are the aliens who have been here for generations; why even my own uncle Percy was a dead ringer for a lizard man. He loved to sit for hours in the sun. Mum always said he was a cold fish and, come to think of it, his skin was somewhat reptilian, always dry and scaly, always peeling off after a sunbake. I remember the last time I was at his house he actually asked me to peel the skin from his back, complaining it was itchy. And I peeled off acres of his damned skin.

I decided to leave those two in the antiques shop. I would study my own family to find the answers to the questions circling around in my head. I was about to cross the road when I took one final peep inside the shop, just in time to see the lizard man poke a reptilian, snake-like tongue out between his lips as if tasting the air and pouf! – in a puff of smoke the two blokes had completely vanished.

I didn't hang about, I can tell you. I was out of there, flat out like a ... no I won't say it but you know what I mean.

I found Uncle Percy sitting on his front veranda in the sun. He was lying on the green and white plastic chaise longue with his hat over his face. I heard a gentle snore coming from beneath the hat. 'Uncle,' I said giving him a shake. 'I think you have fallen asleep in the sun. You are going to get awfully sunburnt if you don't get into the shade pretty soon.'

'What, what!' he cried, waking with a start. 'I was just in the middle of a wonderful dream. I dreamt I was an alien reptile from outer space and I could annihilate anyone who bothered me by just opening my mouth and flicking out my snake tongue like this.'

I ran screaming down the steps, off the veranda, grabbed my bike and was out of there in a flash.

Mrs T – 20 June 1985

Robin Hammond

Sunlight cuts through cold morning air
as she slips along the frost-slick path
to Dangar Falls.
Magpies string along the wires like beads
and far below wood ducks, legs askew
lurch and dip crazily
sliding into the ice-strewn pond.

Mrs T, third-grade teacher at Fairview Primary
family woman, pillar of the community,
pauses on the brink, then
briefly joins the eagles
as arms out she drops
through fog-laden air
to the rock-studded water below –

and around the canyon rim
the winter trees
crystals dripping from their fingers
bow like black skeletons in icy shrouds.

Payback

Diane Jensen

(I acknowledge country of the indigenous desert nation in the Northeast of W.A.)

A watery sun was poking its way from behind distant, purple-hued ranges across the desert.

Jessie Ngarra woke from her troubled sleep. Today was Payback day. She knew the spears would be ready and she knew the boy would be trembling in his hut. This was their lore, and this was his punishment. He had killed two other young men. The wrecked Land Rover, dragged into the community from the desert, was behind the spearing area. Darkened blood smears were visible, inside and out.

From the extended families of the dead, mournful wailing, interspersed with louder cries, split the air throughout the community. For three days they had been mourning. It would continue until well after Payback was over. The dead boys' names rattled around in Jessie's head, but would never be spoken aloud. This was the way.

No police involved in this one. Tribal lore takes care of its own in the desert.

Jessie roughly pushed aside the three dogs from her bed of blankets and old quilts. Their use was over for now. They'd kept her warm in the zero temperatures of the desert night. The *gadiya* always laughed at 'three-dog night' or 'four-dog night' when they passed through the community, buying paintings. No *gadiya* would be here today. It was arranged. At each end of the community stood an ochre-painted tribal member, on the hardened four-wheel drive track which passed through from east to west.

Clambering off the bed on the concrete veranda, Jessie rearranged her voluminous skirt around wide hips. It trailed in the dust. Her multi-coloured, ragged jumper was spattered with spilt food and clinging dog hair; hardly warm enough for a chill desert morning. Grey, unkempt, springy hair poked out at all angles from the old local football team beanie, clamped on her head. Her brown, wrinkled skin was dry and scaly, but her deep eyes were brilliant and ancient, full of knowledge and wisdom. Jessie was a community elder held in great reverence. Today she was sad and shamed. She hoped the boy would be strong and brave, when he walked between the two lines of spears.

She shuffled wearily over, to stir the dying embers of the fire back into life, muttering and scolding the dogs impeding her progress. Hunkered down, once the fire had regained life, Jessie dropped a few more sticks onto it, and gazed across the vast expanse of desert. Slowly,

the day lightened with early morning sun. Her dogs spread out at a cautious distance, watching intently. They knew it would soon be time for food, and settled patiently. Once the food was produced, they would fight viciously over it, but for now they were uneasy mates, resigned to their patient wait.

Jessie lowered the billy to the fire and lifted the heavy lid of a large cast iron pot. The dogs were immediately alert.

'You fellas lucky today,' she said, tossing three bones to them. 'No argue!' she shouted. 'There bone for you each.' But of course they snapped and fought. Jessie left them to it and wandered over to the big communal hand pump. She sluiced water over her face, growling. 'Dem bloody kids make big puddle of water 'ere. Oh well, I wash me feet.'

Collecting her ochre pot, she pumped a little water in and mixed the white ochre to a paste. Applying stripes across her cheeks and forehead, she then lifted her skirt and pasted dabs of ochre on her legs. *Dat enough for now,* she thought.

Back at the fire she threw handfuls of tea into the billy, found her big tin mug and settled back.

The men chosen to sing and dance for the beginning of the Payback ceremony were painted and ready to perform. They dribbled over to the ceremonial area. Those with the punishment spears eventually followed. Jessie stayed where she was and began to croon. She saw there were several with spears so they would form two lines between which the boy would walk. She had hoped there might be only one who was spearing, but the boy had committed a very bad crime and so, as customary lore stated, there were more spears.

This blackfella lore, good lore, teach 'em good, Jessie thought. *Customary lore. No good in gaol* gadiya *way. Dey come out worse off.*

The boy had stolen the Land Rover ute after sniffing petrol. He had persuaded the other two boys to joy-ride with him. He drove a long way into the desert at fast speed. The vehicle, out of control, hit a 200-centimetre solid ant-hill and rolled over many times. Why he was chosen to live, without any severe injuries, amazed him and the people of his community. The vehicle he took was a community vehicle for hunting and picking up stores from Halls Creek. Now they couldn't go hunting or collect stores until another Land Rover was fixed in the workshop. And two boys dead.

Eventually, the singing began, then dancing, clap sticks and didgeridoo timing the dancers while the wailing built to a crescendo. Dust, stirred up by the dancers, lifted, drifting across the community.

As the sun rose higher, warming the day, other community members gathered. All had striped their faces and legs with the ochre. Children, sombre, hanging back, were also painted in ochre. They understood this day and would remember what happens when lore is broken. This – a good thing.

Hot Rocks

Charlie Yangarra, a well-respected elder with good bush medicine skills, was chosen to take care of the boy when it was all over. He too was painted in ochre and with the ceremonial tails and bush turkey feathers tucked into the red band around his waist and head. He would stay with the boy in a special men's place until the boy mended.

Jessie waited. She poked at her fire and filled the tin mug again with tea. Looking to the ranges, but not seeing them, she retreated into dreaming time in her head and continued crooning softly.

Time passed and the singing stopped. The dancers retreated. Jessie, still beside her fire, ceased crooning and turned her head to the gathering. Those who were spearing, assembled in two lines, several feet apart from each other. The wailing quieted and the boy was brought out. Jessie turned away. Again, she hoped the boy would be strong and brave.

Angry shouts in language, of the boy's deeds intermingled with renewed wailing, as the clap sticks sounded out again. The boy began walking between the lines. The spears each found their mark directed at his thighs. As the spears fell out, blood flowed from his body. He stumbled, but straightened again, looking ahead. He was strong, accepting his punishment bravely, though trembling and weakened. Blood poured from the more vengeful, deepest wounds, turning his legs bright crimson.

Then it was over. The community hushed.

Jessie shifted a little, settled, and relaxed. Mngarri, her sister, walked over to her and sat down beside her.

'That old Charlie got him now,' she said. 'He take care of him.' Jessie nodded. Mngarri reached for the billy and put it back on the smouldering fire.

'He done good Jessie. He done real good, your boy. You get 'im back your boy, real soon.'

Love

Margaret Drury

The girl I love is like an exquisite, sweet-scented rose. She stands out in a crowd as tall and slender as an arum lily.

I have seen him looking at me with his brown, liquid chocolate eyes. He is so well built, muscular and handsome. He reminds me of a mighty tree or majestic stag. I blush from head to toe when he looks my way. I was so excited to be invited to a banquet in his castle and he seated me on his right side. He has asked father for my hand in marriage, and was so attentive to me, bringing figs and raisins and other lovely gifts and flowers from his glasshouse. Now he has gone far away into the hills on a hunting trip and I am left to languish, longing for his return. I think I hear his voice calling to me from the mountains and can see him in the distance. No, it is a stag, with magnificent horns leaping from rock to rock, yet somehow it materialises into my love. He comes and looks through the garden to where I am waiting and says:

'Come away with me and we will have a spring wedding. There are flowers blooming everywhere and the birds are singing and building nests. All the fruit trees and vines on my estate are bearing fruit. We can have a wonderful honeymoon wherever you choose, then return to enjoy the riches I have worked for.'

Hot Rocks

Who would think he could be as gentle as a young deer drinking daintily from a pool, yet strong as the mighty stag with its long antlers, surveying its kingdom.

My love is like a dove hiding in the trees. Her voice is as sweet as her face. She is like honey but as fragile as fine porcelain. I am almost afraid to hug her in case she breaks. I am so big and clumsy. I now have to lay traps for the little foxes, who are worrying the sheep and spoiling the tender grapes on my vines. If I don't do this there will be no banquets for our families and friends.

I love my beloved so much and I know he is mine! He is like a shepherd looking after everything on his estate including me. His sheep graze among the lilies. I wish I could go hunting with him in the mountains. I must wait patiently for his return with some venison. It seems a pity to kill such beautiful creatures but my love says he must cull them, so I do not protest anymore.

Enemy on the Water

Craig Slobin

Young Dara smiled from the end of the war party as they trudged over the purple heathers. The jests were a pleasant way to keep their minds on other things. More to the point, it was a good way to keep their mind off one thing in particular; the upcoming battle.

Nobody was sure where or when the fight would take place, but wherever and whenever, each and every hour took them closer to both: to their survival, or their doom.

King Seamus's army of five-hundred was travelling in bands of ten warriors: fifty war bands loosely grouped and spread out over the hills and dales as they trudged ever onwards, towards the coast. Even their king did not know the might of the enemy, yet surely this force was enough. All of King Seamus's liege lords had answered his call to arms. They had gathered with their best and most famous warriors, and a handful of boys like Dara, to make their numbers greater.

Of course, King Seamus was only one king in a land of many. Not that this army was looking for a tussle with any of its neighbours. No, the enemy they hunted had come across the seas. Two years ago was the first time the foreign invaders had appeared on these shores, burning, raping and looting wherever they went. None of the Kings of Erin had been prepared for such carnage to their peoples and clans; nor the speed with which it had happened. In but five days the clans on the coast who had been attacked were slaughtered; or their people stolen, if female and of child-bearing age.

The next year had been the same. The invaders had landed further up the coast last summer and repeated their brutish behaviour with other clans. It was said they spoke an alien tongue and were twice as large as normal men, that they rowed their longboats for countless miles upon miles across the stormy seas and used giant axes instead of swords.

Well, this year would be different. This year King Seamus was prepared and ready. At the first sign of longboats on the horizon the king of this land had marshalled his best and finest warriors to meet them head-on in the field, with a handful of boys to add to their numbers. Boys like Dara, whose family owned a sword. It was his dead grandfather's weapon from the past, but the leader of this war band, Cohan, said it would suffice. This summer, King Seamus was ready and waiting. This summer, the People of Erin would throw the foreign, warlike giants back into the northern seas.

Dara was the youngest by far in this war band, maybe even the youngest in King Seamus's army, at thirteen. He was afraid, but glad of his comrades' brave humour and proud wit. This game of jests was keeping his mind on fictional happy things, and not the dreadful scary things of reality. Like his death which may lie just over the next hill or down the next dale.

'No, I told her, I want to wet my other wick!' Liam ended his jest with the punchline.

'And?!' asked Hamish with a grin.

'And, my dearest Hamish,' continued Liam with a smug smile. 'She burned it all night long!' The war band roared with laughter.

Dara frowned from the back. 'I don't get it,' he admitted. His freckled cheeks flushed when the others all chuckled. Though these brave warriors made him feel safer, he also felt like an imposter around such great men, especially when he did not understand something they said, even more so when they all laughed without him.

Cohan, who was leading, smiled at Dara like an older brother. He was not the only one to treat him so; the entire war party treated short Dara like a younger sibling and often ruffled up his curly red hair. Dara was not the only one without a helmet either. In fact, only five of the ten wore helmets and even fewer had a chainmail shirt. Dara had neither luxury. Indeed, his family sword was rather small and slender, compared to the others'.

'You will understand soon enough, lad,' said Cohan with a crooked grin. 'Mayhap, when we defeat these alien monsters, we should all take little Dara to the capital and pay a woman for him.'

The band laughed loudly again and Dara blushed anew. Liam paused until Dara was beside him, and slapped his back. 'It's decided, lads! If little Dara be old enough to fight these savage barbarians, then he be old enough to wet his wick if he lives!'

Hamish grinned at him from further in front. 'Aye, little Dara, you be a brave lad, you be. But let's hope your cock not be as small as that sword of yours, hey?'

Big Patrick, who was the tallest and strongest of this band, not to mention the oldest, at forty, chuckled. 'Don't you worry none, little Dara, even if you do be little down there,' he advised with wisdom. 'It be what you do with it that counts, laddie, not its size.' As the others all ribbed Patrick, teasing that he must have a small dick to have said such, Dara sighed with relief. Honestly, he did not know if his manhood was big or small compared to others, but if it was small Patrick gave him some hope.

'Done then!' Cohan cut in on the bullying banter aimed at big Patrick. 'It's been decided, little Dara. After we push these giant bastards back into the sea, we lot will head for the capital and buy you a romp. What do you say to that, lad?'

'Um, thank you.' What was he supposed to say? Besides, all this talk of losing his virginity was exciting him, small penis or not. 'Um, none of you will tell my mammy though, will you?' The hillside erupted with harsh laughter again and Dara's curly, red hair got mussed up again by most of them.

***

The scent of smoke on the air was their first warning. The gut-wrenching death screams of men, women and children their second. Dara slid up the small rise with the others in his band amongst all of the war parties. The five hundred warriors were silent and still for the most part. They watched and waited with trepidation and adrenaline both.

Dara's deep blue eyes could finally see the carnage when he reached the top and his gasp was loud and frightened. Down below was a large village, and it burned. Clan folk shouted and screamed, some trying to flee while others attempted to fight the huge men destroying their homes and people. Through the thick, acrid smoke he saw a young boy chopped in half by a giant using a huge axe, and a woman being raped in the dirt while being held by two others. A brave, unarmed man fought to save her but another giant simply reached out and snapped his neck with his bare hands. Then he saw the most horrid crime in the world. One of the enemy invaders picked up a squealing Erin bairn from the dirt by a foot, and tossing the poor thing into one of the many fires of the burning houses.

Everywhere he looked was carnage. And these large men in armour shirts and with big round shields were grinning manically as they carried out their destruction of the once-peaceful village. They howled with laughter and their icy eyes glinted with excitement while they brought hell on earth to these People of Erin.

Finding a moment of courage, Dara counted the giant long-haired and long-bearded men; men with rippling muscles, hair of yellow-gold and eyes of brilliant blue. They were demons surely, yet they looked as beautiful and strong as angels as they wreaked their suffering. He counted two-hundred at the least, but knew there must be more, for the sandy beach beside them held many, many longboats; boats big enough to carry twice that many devils.

As he lay there shivering and trembling, with untold horror and dread, word came down the long line of warriors. Dara was unsure how he felt about the orders given his own war band and some others.

'Right, lads!' whispered Cohan fiercely, though the noise below meant he could have shouted and not been heard by the enemy. 'Slide back down! To the beach! To the beach! Liam, Hamish! Get a fire going in the dunes! You others make torches from driftwood and seaweed!' His eyes were alight with anger and retribution. 'Patrick, you big bastard! You lead with me!'

The band sneaked back down the slope and off towards the beach. Dara glanced behind to see five other war bands doing the same. He hoped those monsters out there did not see them too soon, the sixty Erin fighters would be massacred if found out. Dara was no war leader, but even he understood what the six bands were about. He could only hope their actions would not doom all of Erin. What if they lost this battle? What if because of their actions these demons from hell were stuck here forever more?

In the dunes, many small fires burst to life, still out of sight from the village. It was awful hard not to act, not to attack despite his fear, what with the villagers screaming and shrieking death cries of pure torture. He was not sure what was worse, the death screeches, or the screams of the women being raped in the dirt and ashes of their homes. Dara held his newly-made torch before him in his left hand; his right tightly clasped his small and slender sword.

'Lads!' called Cohan, to all six war bands scattered over the sands. 'Light your brands!' He nodded at everyone, even giving Dara a wink to try to ease his panic. 'Go! Go, go, go!'

Dara lit his torch with a shaking arm, took a deep breath and took off in a sprint to keep up with Cohan and Patrick. The soft sands slowed him down and his breaths grew laboured, but only until he hit the hard, wet sand below the tide line. In his adrenaline-filled run he soon found himself in the lead with another young lad. The others of the war bands were heavier of foot and slower to reach the longboats.

Hot Rocks

Being first as he was now, he sprinted all the way to the furthest boat with his young comrade. When they reached the low-sided, beautifully-carved vessel, they wasted no time in searching out some material within. It seemed these demonic giants did not row all the way from whatever hell they came from, for covering every oar bench was a large sail. Dara nodded at his accomplice and they launched their firebrands on top of the skin sail; and with a great, whoosh, it went up in flames. Their mission accomplished, Dara searched out the many boats to see flames licking every one of them. The sails within were causing huge billows of black smoke to rise and he realised they had been seen.

From the village came a monstrous roar, many bellows of fury and spite. He quickly yanked his offsider's hand, pulling him along behind him, but not quickly enough. Not fast enough to beat these giant men in a foot race. His heart truly stopped when he saw several blond-headed, blue-eyed savages ploughing through the white sands towards them. Behind the enemies still in the village, King Seamus's ram horn trumpeted out, followed by the fierce roar of four-hundred and forty Warriors of Erin.

Dara saw King Seamus leading the charge, but then his vision was filled with long, plaited hair and beards, and snarling faces, screaming at him in alien words. He turned to fight, even though these foreigners were five times as big as he, and five times stronger. The two young Erin men stood side-by-side to face what was coming. And Dara knew his end was near. They were gigantic men, with muscles that bulged and contracted with power. With nothing left him but bravery, he screamed back at them and charged head first at the closest giant. He slipped on some seaweed and it surely saved his life. His companion was not so lucky. When Dara hit the sand his friend was left alone and with one quick slash of his battle axe the foreigner took the other boy's head clean off.

The enemy demon howled with delight, smiled a savage grin at Dara lying on the beach, and attacked. In his haste to get at him, he too slipped on the slimy weed, and when he landed beside Dara, waves of sand erupted. Dara cried out in shock and fear, and lashed out with his tiny sword. With eyes as wide as they could surely go, he watched in fascination as his sword point bit into the giant's neck and blood spewed out. The next thing he knew, other Warriors of Erin were rushing by him to meet the foe from this side while King Seamus struck the other.

Dara gazed at the man he had stabbed. He watched the blood flow, soaking his huge, blond beard. He stared in wonder as the giant's piercing blue eyes faded, and he did not know how he felt about it. At first he felt remorse, but it was quickly replaced by relief and joy. Especially when he found his feet to discover his king and warriors had won. His war band found him and raised him up on their shoulders, promising he would be a man by the end of the week. Dara was happy, very happy. His only moment of worry was: what would happen next year when the giants returned again? He really should acquire a bigger sword.

Lost and Found

Denise Delaney

She was five when first she lost her leg.

A chortling girl child skipped and slid in the mud, hit a patch of clay and with a swoosh and an electric jolt she slammed onto the ground.

She tried to stand and, failing, realised her leg had gone. Panic rising, she scuffled around in the mud but could neither feel nor see it. She sat back in stunned silence as the cows formed a circle of concern at this oddity in their midst.

She blacked out when the pain intruded and came to, in the bath. In growing horror, she looked at the lumpy purple swollen thing attached at her thigh. 'Not my leg. That's not my leg. You have to find my leg!'

Her mother protested, was rational and logical, then prodded and poked, but she knew that this alien thing had been stitched on while she was senseless. Her father tried humour, baby tricks of thumbs and noses taken off and put back on, then gave in to her pleas and went back to search the yard. On his return, empty-handed, she became louder and more shrill, and every breath was a huge airsucking sob of denial.

She was sedated and slowly calmed.

Hot Rocks

On the way to bed she dimly heard Grandad offering crutches and a wooden leg for his little 'Twinkletoes'. The crutches were presented the next morning and adjusted to fit, then Grandad took measurements of her remaining leg, went to his woodpile, where he selected a branch about the right size and shape and began whittling, the wood shavings making a soft moving blanket on and around him.

She quickly became adept with crutches, swinging up and down stairs and manouevring over uneven ground and through tufty grass then, gaining confidence, she found the pleasures of flying through the air, flinging her body higher and higher, circling on a wooden point, creating three-legged polkas and pirouettes. A human ... brolga ... lightness that faded quickly when the sun went down.

Nights were difficult. She had terrifying dreams of drowning in many-coloured, multi-legged jellies with unblinking black eyes. She began sleepwalking. One midnight trek found her in the sewing room, a hand clutching the sharp scissors, the other pulling out the skin at the thigh, attempting to cut off this now yellow-and-green monstrosity.

With time, however, the nightmares did recede and her feet did become still during sleep.

Finally, the 'Fitting of The Wooden Leg' day arrived. She awoke, her daylight dancing fingers counting: 'Eyes ... one, two. Nose ... one. Mouth ... one. Ears ... one, two. Arms ... one, two. Leg... one ... two.' She flung off the bedclothes and there it was, bland, normal, right size, right shape. She flexed her knee, ankle and toes and everything worked.

The alien, sometime during that night, had gone away.

She was twelve when next she lost her leg.

The Irish/Scottish Wedding

Terry Dunkley

Coleen O'Malley came from a good Irish Catholic family, while the bridegroom, Hamish Campbell, came from a good Scottish Presbyterian family. Not that either family was particularly religious; neither were they regular churchgoers but out of custom the O'Malleys always ate fish on Fridays while the Campbells claimed to eat anything on Fridays as long as it was meat.

The O'Malleys desired Coleen to marry a nice Catholic boy, as long as he was not Spanish or Italian, while the Campbells wanted Hamish to marry a nice Presbyterian girl, preferably with a Scottish heritage. But Eros had fired his arrows into Coleen and Hamish when they had first met, and they had been inseparable ever since.

Despite family resentments, their love was so great it surmounted everything and everyone who tried to come between them, and believe me, there was quite a bit to overcome. But they were both over twenty-one years of age and made their own decisions in life. In order not to provoke either side on their religious views, they arranged for a civil marriage ceremony to be conducted by a local celebrant. It was a touching ceremony, during which the celebrant pronounced them husband and wife. Then they were conveyed to the Headland for their photo shoot, while all the guests retired to the Seabreeze Hotel to while away an hour before the reception. Sadly, the O'Malleys stayed on one side of the pub while the Campbells stayed on the other. It was as if neither side would make any effort to integrate.

Now at the wedding reception, the division still remained. Waiters moved through the throng with glasses of wine, champagne and Jameson Irish whiskey. The Irish homed in on the whisky and so did the Scots, complaining that at a decent wedding reception they would have served a good scotch like Black Douglas or Chivas Regal instead of that Irish stuff. By the time the wedding breakfast was in full swing, it appeared that all the men plus some of the women were well into their cups. Then after the main course, it was time for the speeches and the father of the bride had his turn. Bryan O'Malley stepped up to the microphone.

'Let me make it clear,' he said. 'I brought my daughter up in the Catholic faith and now she has married someone outside of the faith and he has made her a dishonourable woman.'

Hamish's father started to rise from his chair but his wife pushed down on his thigh and stopped him. 'Angus, I know how you feel, but don't spoil this special day.'

Eventually it was Angus's turn to speak. 'Angus,' she said. 'Let it go. It's our son's wedding day, don't spoil it.'

'I'll get that Irish bastard before the night's out! I swear it.'

'Let me say,' he began, 'in reply to the bog Irishman that produced a daughter of far greater intelligence than himself, she is an honourable woman in the eyes of God and of the laws of this great land, and the Papists have no say in this matter.' Then, upon concluding his speech, he walked past Bryan O'Malley's table, leaned towards him and said, 'How was that you Irish pig?' With a deft move of his hand, he knocked a near-full glass of Guinness into his lap.

Bryan O'Malley leapt to his feet. 'You porridge-faced Scotsman,' he yelled. 'Take this!' He threw a punch at his face. It was a quick jab that landed squarely on Angus's nose, a stinging blow that made his eyes water and his anger rise. O'Malley's wife was now hanging onto her husband's back.

'No! No!' she screamed. 'Not here Bryan, not on Coleen's wedding day!' Angus's wife had also come in to calm things down and wrapped her arms tightly around him so that he could not strike back, which gave Bryan O'Malley the opportunity to get another two hits in. It was at this moment that Angus resented his wife's intervention. He was fired-up on whisky and she was holding him back from what he needed to do. Shrugging her off, he charged back at O'Malley, but something had changed. O'Malley was surrounded by five of his sons.

Hot Rocks

At this point, the Campbell sons came into play. One of them picked up a water jug and smashed it over the head of one of the O'Malley boys, leaving an equal balance of four against four; but the guests were now taking sides, with uncles and cousins rising from their seats, and those that chose to step back were very few.

Coleen and Hamish just looked at each other, and in that beautiful, silent communication that flows between lovers, slipped away. Their bags were packed and in the boot of Hamish's car, ready to leave for their two-week honeymoon at an undisclosed destination. They both laughed uproariously as two police cars with lights flashing and sirens wailing passed them, going in the direction from which they had both come.

'You know Coleen, we never did have our bridal waltz, but we've got a whole lifetime ahead to catch up on that. Meanwhile, tonight the police are going to have a merry dance, just for you and me.'

Hot Rocks

Postcard from New York

Denise Delaney

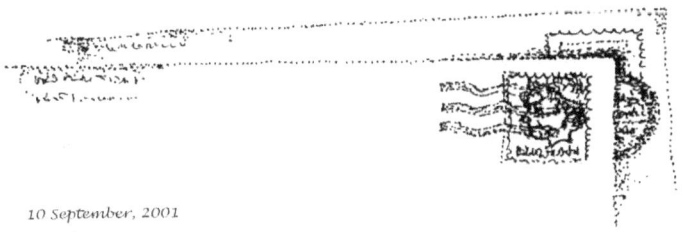

10 September, 2001

Dear Mum,

    We made it. Halfway around the world and the 'Big Apple' is as full of people as I expected. We had a great lunch at the 90th floor of one of their Twin Towers.

    We thought we'd have a daily ritual of breakfast up on the Towers, then a leisurely walk to the tennis, with the hope our little Aussie battler comes away with the win, so will be doing that tomorrow.

    Talk to you when we get to London.

    Love David.

The Proposition

Christopher Hammond

I was 17 years old and, although it took me many years to realise it, I was smoking hot. I was living with a friend in Forest Lodge, an inner Sydney suburb, in a filthy house with holes in the floor, roof, sink and bath. The previous owner had covered the walls in an attractive nicotine-yellow, by smoking 70 high-tar cigarettes a day, until he keeled over and died in what was now my bedroom. In the years I lived there, I was unable to remove the bloodstains from the floorboards, although admittedly I didn't try too hard.

We were living there rent-free because we were supposed to be renovating the house. The dwelling was perched precariously on a hill overlooking the Harold Park Raceway, where I first met Ruth. She was an elegant lady, of mature years and devastatingly attractive.

It was not exactly love at first sight but a good deal of lust was involved. I courted her for weeks. I even spent several chaste evenings on her couch just so I could wake up and cook her a good breakfast. I was smitten.

Of course, when I invited Ruth to a romantic dinner at my house, I really should have known better. It was a small miracle she managed to avoid falling through the numerous holes in the floor. Perhaps, more than anything, it was the proliferation of insect life that spoiled the atmosphere. It's somewhat difficult to court a sophisticated, silver-haired siren while every variety of nocturnal insect is propelling itself energetically through the non-existent floorboards of your dining room.

We went to the pub the next day and I figured I'd done all I possibly could to woo her. Besides, how difficult could it be to convince a 50-year old woman, no matter how attractive, to jump into the sack with a tall, 17 year-old blue-eyed, blond, hottie?

Not just difficult but impossible, it turned out.

I duly propositioned her. She fixed me with an amused gaze: 'I'm afraid, little boy, you just couldn't handle me.'

My shoulders, which were, only a moment before, enormous and manly (obviously not so irresistibly manly as I had imagined) slumped considerably. I cringed and shuffled away, back to my life of insect-ridden decrepitude. It was probably for the best. I'm not really sure how I would have explained the bloodstains all over my bedroom floor.

I Quit

Lucy Powter

I was crying as I threw everything into my bags. I had found a lift with a person who was prepared to drive me to the railway station so I could go back home. I left the keys with the lady next door to our dress shop with a mumbled explanation and took off home. I was running away and feeling terrible that I had let Madam down and couldn't tell her why. During the trip home, I thought about the last year.

I was 17 and had finished school the year before and felt unsettled, so mum suggested I go and visit a friend of hers, a widow Katrina Shapski, and her daughter Rose, who lived about three hours away in a small town. According to Mum, she had built her own home, bit by bit. Intrigued, I went. Mum's friend greeted me warmly. Even though her house was full of people, she made a bed for me in the lounge room. Rose and I explored the town the next day, where I noticed an ad in the window of an exclusive dress shop for a young shop assistant. So, on an impulse, I applied.

My interview was with the owner, a lady with lovely black neatly coiffured hair, wearing a black check, well-cut modern suit with fashionable jewellery and black high-heeled shoes. Her face was pale and she wore makeup which was well applied, with bright red lipstick. She appeared to be about 40, with a full figure, and insisted I call her 'Madam'. There was something about her I liked straight away. She explained what my position would entail, such as working in the shop, selling and getting the season's clothes ready for the mannequin parades she and I would organise, using local models. I had always loved clothes and now I would be able to see what was fashionable and available for the coming season.

I was delighted to get the job and began looking for accommodation, which I found with an acquaintance of Mrs Shapski. So with Rose's help, I moved into my room and began work the next day. After a few busy days, I met Madam's husband Levi. He was a short man of slim build, wearing an elegant, pale grey suit with a white polo-necked jumper and black, highly polished shoes. He appeared to be the same age as Madam. I learnt that he did the shop's books each week and that he worked from home as he looked after their eight-year-old son.

I had started work in between seasons, so I had some time in the shop learning how to run it, how to dress the front window and to pick up and display the clothes that Madam would choose on her biannual buying trips to Sydney. I watched and learned how Madam picked her models from local women who frequented the shop, who were the size she was looking for, and how she would teach them to walk on the catwalk displaying the clothes so elegantly. I was very excited to learn how to assemble the clothes and accessories that Madam wanted the models to wear and how to transport them out of town.

My first mannequin parade was in our small town and there was a flurry of chosen outfits to prepare and make ready for the day, accessories to pick out and jewellery to add. It was so exciting! I was on such a high and delighted that Madam trusted me to look after it all. The parade and refreshments Madam had ordered from one of the local cafes went off very well.

There was a huge crowd on the day and we had lots of orders coming in. Madam was pleased. I was very busy in the coming weeks but noticed that Levi was coming into the shop much more often. What he said and how he looked at me, made me feel very uncomfortable but I dismissed it, thinking maybe I hadn't heard him properly or he was joking. I tried to forget, as I had such admiration for his wife and her future plans for the shop, which she had shared with me over coffee.

It was time to take the parade out of town and it was my job to make sure the clothes were clean and everything was ready to pack into the shop's van. Levi and I packed the van and I noticed he was smiling a lot and touching me at every opportunity. During the journey, which was an hour's drive, he asked if I knew what a mistress was and explained how he could set me up in a new flat with all the clothes I wanted. I just had to be nice to him. I felt sick, I didn't know what to do. Who could I tell? He knew I couldn't or wouldn't tell Madam. I thought I may have imagined the whole thing and tried focusing on the order book and models' outfits which I had written down, noting the accessories that went with each of the outfits. So I didn't hear or ignored most of what Levi was saying to me.

The parade went off well and we had one of the models join us for the drive home, which was very pleasant as she was so excited and talked most of the way home. I tried very hard not to think about what Levi had said to me.

After the success of the parade, Madam told me the lady for the small sizes was leaving town and asked me to model them. My happiness was complete. She spent a lot of time teaching me how to walk and carry myself on the catwalk and how to apply makeup correctly. She picked out the outfits she wanted me to model, with all the paraphernalia that went with it. It was such an exciting time, I forgot about how uncomfortable I was when her husband came into the shop, and I learnt how to keep out of his clutches. Oh, how the weeks went by, and my first outing on the catwalk went off without any problems. It was wonderful!

However, things began to spiral out of control in the coming weeks. I had great difficulty keeping out of reach of Levi's arms. He would try to pin me against the wall in the office or come up behind me; his hands were demanding more. I felt bad, as if it was my fault. Was I maybe encouraging him? I couldn't look Madam in the eye or tell anyone, even Rose, who had become a good friend, just in case she told someone else. It was a small town and I did not want to ruin Madam's reputation. Thus I came up with the plan of running away.

Mum met me at the railway station and when we were home, I told her everything, in between tears, hiccups, hugs and coffee. We never heard anything from Madam or anyone from that town.

Ode to Gout

Craig Slobin

Gout, gout, bloody gout,
I just can't work it out,
I've had no beer or spirits, or even a bloody stout,
But I've got it yet again, this damned bloody gout
Gout, gout, silly, stupid gout.

I went to the chemist, to see what he had to tout,
He remembered me from my last bout of gout,
'Stop drinking!' he commanded, with an angry shout,
But I hadn't been drinking, the silly bloody lout,
I was so upset I almost gave him a good clout,
Doesn't matter anyway, even when I don't drink I still get gout,
Gout, gout, stupid bloody gout.

I suppose that means he too can't figure it out,
I wonder what it's all about;
Reckon if I was a priest I wouldn't get it, not if I was devout,
And as for grog, I'll just have to do without,
That's certainly something I won't flout about,
Stupid, stupid, bloody gout.

I've hit a wall of confusion and pain, I'm in a complete rout,
A wall that's falling apart, like dunny tiles with no grout,
Oh well, I'll just have to suck it up until I work it out,
Bugger me, I hate fucking gout!

Angel

Robin Hammond

Night had fallen and we were almost home when the storm struck. Lightning flashed and flickered all around us and, within minutes, the old DC3 we'd chartered to get us back to Rabaul was being tossed about like a feather. The eerie and familiar glow of Vulcan and its red rim of lava, seemed almost close enough to touch.

'Fuuuck!' groaned Ralph. He turned green and buried his head in the vomit bag. I gulped down a big glass of vodka, crossed every finger and looked around at our friends and fellow passengers. Their faces were all anxious, and so was the pilot's. Our club having at last won the weekend squash tournament against bitter rivals Port Moresby, we'd all been thoroughly pissed when we boarded. There'd been much raucous singing and toasting and staggering up and down the aisle. Now we'd all gone quiet.

'We can't land,' called out the pilot, 'too much water on the runway. We'll have to circle and hope to god we've got enough fuel.' I sent up a prayer. Why, oh why, had we left our cosy inner-city bungalow in Melbourne to come to this?

This was New Guinea in the 1960s and we were living the dream. We'd landed cushy jobs in the last decade of

Hot Rocks

Australian colonialism. We lolled away our days at desks beneath softly clicking ceiling fans. Black underlings did the heavy lifting, calling us 'master' and 'missus' with all the deference they could muster. We spent evenings at the Rabaul Yacht Club, stubbies in hand, with black waiters in bright-coloured lap-laps attending to our every imperious need. On weekends, we idled by the pool at our luxury company home while black *haus bois* polished, scrubbed, laundered and ironed. They left at dusk, gratefully clutching the few dollars we paid them for two ten-hour days of hard slog.

'Tenkyu masta. Tenkyu missis'. They'd bob their woolly heads as they edged away, back into their strange tribal lives.

'What would we do without them?' I always said to Ralphie, as I went around disinfecting the doorknobs, the only cleaning I ever had to do for myself.

Occasionally, we stirred ourselves out of our torpor to fly to Madang, Lae or Port Moresby on chartered flights for a weekend of a bit of squash and lots of booze, which is what we'd been doing on this occasion. I peered into the gloom: lightning flashed, rain pelted down and the plane jerked and shuddered. I was terrified. I swigged some more vodka.

Then, to my horror, I noticed the wing beginning to break loose from the plane! I grabbed Ralph's sleeve.

'Ralphie! Look, the wing's breaking off!' He peered blearily out the window for a second then returned to his sick bag.

'At least it'll be quick,' he mumbled.

I couldn't believe it. He didn't seem to care! I was just about to alert the pilot when I saw something even more astonishing. There was a figure – it looked like a man – on the wing, out there in the raging tempest. He wore gloves and a full-face helmet and carried a welding pack. He knelt down and began welding that wing back onto the plane! I tried to get Ralph to look but he was busy throwing up and when he finally did, he said he couldn't see anything.

I couldn't take my eyes off this figure working away on the wing. When he finished, he stood up, pulled off his gloves, lifted his helmet, looked straight at me and produced a dazzling smile. Then, I'm not kidding, he turned around and an enormous pair of golden wings unfolded from the back of those overalls and he flapped away through the stormy clouds. And like a miracle, the storm just stopped dead and a clear, starry sky hung over everything. The plane landed safely, we taxied to the terminal and piled out, laughing with relief.

I was raised a Catholic, so I'm easily convinced on matters spiritual but that sure gave me pause for thought. An angel – in a welding suit – and I haven't told you the best of it yet. When he lifted off that helmet and revealed his black frizzy hair and his very dark skin, I was dumbfounded. He was black – a black angel! I'd never heard of such a thing.

But then, when I thought about it, it made sense. After all, this was New Guinea, and we had to have someone for all the messy jobs, didn't we?

It made me think about things, though, and next weekend I added another dollar to our *haus bois'* paypackets. Yes, I know it seems extravagant but as I always said to Ralphie: 'What would we do without them?'

The Dark Brown Suit

Barbara Harvey

The skiff drifted along in rhythm with the gentle flow of the river. Ruth snuggled back, eyes closed, face to the sun, enjoying the feel of the tender rocking of the little vessel. She could just hear the happy voices of the children running and playing on the riverbank as her senses caught the fragrance of wild flowers growing alongside the river. She couldn't place the flora to which this perfume belonged but felt she had smelled it before. Ruth could hear a distant buzzing but was not worried she would be drifting into a swarm of bees.

How could anyone worry on a day like today?

However, the buzzing became louder, causing Ruth to turn and lazily open her eyes to discover its source. It took a few seconds to focus until she could clearly see the brown wardrobe door to the side of her, the buzzing being the alarm clock in its attempt to remind her she needed to get up and get ready for work. She switched off the alarm and sank back into her pillows trying to recapture the dream, but it had faded away.

She felt warm and cosy but as she stretched her legs they met with cold sheets, reminding her that Michael would have left a while ago. She rolled over and could still just feel the imprint of his body on the mattress. They seemed to be like ships in the night these days, passing each other infrequently as life moved on.

Ruth showered and dressed in her uniform, made the bed and went downstairs to see to a few chores before heading out to work. Running the hot water into the kitchen sink, she noticed with irritation that yet again, Michael had placed the cereal bowl in the sink without leaving it soaking and now the leftover cereal bits had gone hard and would be more difficult to remove. There were toast crumbs on the breadboard, an invitation to the ants that breakfast was awaiting them. How many times had she asked Michael to not do this? His reasoning was that he didn't want to wake her with the clatter of breakfast dishes in the sink. So, each morning she had to face the task of washing the breakfast things, and usually she was okay about this but today it seemed to annoy her more than usual.

A while later, she left for work. It would be another long day in the hospital wards and she would not be home much before 11 pm. Michael would by then have gone to bed, his work day starting early. Today, she had a few household errands to run before heading into work to begin her shift.

The traffic seemed to be particularly heavy this morning and soon she'd caught up with a traffic jam. As she sat waiting for the vehicles ahead to move, she glanced across the road at the bus stop. There were a few people waiting, just ordinary folk, and yet one person seemed to stand out. He was tall – she thought about Michael's height – and was wearing a very well-fitting dark brown suit, unusual for this area. On his head was a beige trilby. She couldn't see his face as his back was turned towards her. Then the traffic moved and he was gone.

Once at work, Ruth went about her routine duties, but throughout the day her mind kept drifting back to that bus queue and the man in the dark brown suit. His body fitted the suit really well and she wondered if he worked out. She'd always admired a man dressed in a suit. Michael didn't own a suit, his opinion being they should only be worn for weddings and funerals. As these were few and far between, what was the point of his having one? He certainly didn't need it for work in the factory.

They lived in Dagenham, near London, and Michael was the manager of a small factory at the other end of town, responsible for about 100 staff members. He seemed to enjoy the work and responsibility but the owners kept a close eye on things, keeping their executive staff on their toes, hence the reason he was out early every morning, never lingering at home. The traffic was always heavy and he didn't want to be late for work.

Ruth felt life had become very mundane; she would have liked some excitement. She missed the snuggles and cuddles they used to enjoy before Michael's promotion and her shift hours made it so they hardly saw much of each other. The weekends were no different – she had housework and shopping to catch up with and Michael was always busy, winter and summer, coaching the under-11s boys' and girls' soccer. Their birds, now grown, had flown the nest and were developing their own lives. Of course, she and Michael had helped them along the way – college fees, cars, house deposits, they didn't begrudge them. She'd taken the permanent late shift to earn that bit extra so they could afford the odd weekend escape or occasional holiday. But that was two-and-a-half years ago and they hadn't managed to do either yet.

A few days later, Ruth again noticed 'The Suit' in the bus queue but she couldn't stare for too long as the traffic was moving. And again, he had on the beige trilby but he was reading a newspaper, so once again she could not see his face. The next day she glanced across to the bus stop but he wasn't there and yet the following Wednesday there he was again, always the dark brown suit and the beige trilby. This continued for a few weeks and Ruth could not help but become intrigued. Why always on Wednesday? Though not always alone; sometimes he was chatting and laughing with a couple of other suited guys. But in all this time she still hadn't been able to catch sight of his face.

As the weeks passed, Ruth became fixated on the bus stop scene and it occupied her thoughts more and more as she went about her routine work. It was no good, she had to see him for herself, up close. Not to speak to, just to have a look. However, her fantasies were beginning to run wild. She built up an Adonis in her imaginings and maybe ... what if ... *Oh! Stop that!* she told herself.

So, the following Tuesday she left work early, having arranged to take the Wednesday off. Michael was surprised when she arrived home before he'd gone to bed, where Ruth usually found him snoring away when she crept in from work late at night.

'We weren't busy so I decided to leave early,' she explained, although Michael hadn't actually asked the reason, being engrossed in watching a movie. 'Also, I've decided to take the day off tomorrow; thought I'd do some window shopping, maybe a bit of retail therapy. I thought I'd take the bus for a change. You can have the car if you want.' She turned and headed for the kitchen. 'I'll put the jug on, make some tea,' she said.

'Okay, that'll be nice,' was Michael's response, looking back at the television now the ads were finished.

As Ruth drank her tea, she tried to imagine the scene. Would he be there alone or with his friends? If he was alone and she stood next to him, she might say hello, or he might speak first. She felt sure they would be attracted to each other; the opposite didn't enter her mind. After all, she had taken care of herself over the years in an attempt to keep her youthful looks and figure. She occasionally caught the twinkle of an eye from a gentleman as he passed her by, so why wouldn't he be attracted to her? What if he asked her out? Would she say yes or no? She didn't want to cheat on Michael, but surely a cup of coffee or a drink in a bar somewhere wouldn't hurt. Her thoughts raced ahead in all directions.

'I'm going up,' she said. 'Get an early night for a change.' She took their empty cups to the kitchen.

'Right, I won't be long, this movie hasn't got far to go and I would like to see the end of it.'

As Ruth climbed the stairs, she thought about what clothes she should wear tomorrow – something sexy, or would that be too forward for a chance meeting? Or something more businesslike, though perhaps a little stuffy. Maybe just a nice summery dress, very casual. She didn't have a lot to choose from; she'd always worn a uniform at work and money wasn't plentiful enough to go splashing around on the latest trends or frivolous outfits. Besides, where would she put lots of clothes? They only had a small wardrobe each. However, she felt sure she could find something suitable, something pretty. She did have a few nice things in Michael's wardrobe that she hadn't worn for a while. Maybe something in there would be suitable. Her clothes had spilled over into his wardrobe over the years.

She sat on the side of the bed, again pondering the possibilities of tomorrow's scenario. She'd wash her hair so it looked shiny and fresh, take extra care with her make-up – something else she didn't have much of, as make-up was frowned on at work. She'd often heard Matron ordering other nurses to remove theirs before entering the wards.

Standing up, she decided to make her decision tonight about what to wear, instead of wasting precious time in the morning and she opened her wardrobe door. As she'd suspected, there was nothing in there that caught her eye so she moved across to Michael's, opened the door and started sifting through the hangers. As she did so, her eyes were attracted to an unfamiliar, yet familiar, sight – a dark brown suit! She carefully lifted it out and studied it, felt it, smelled it. *I'm sure I've smelled that sweetness before*, she thought but couldn't place the where and when.

She carefully returned the suit to its place but looked up to the shelf above and there it was – a beige trilby. Ruth slowly went downstairs.

'Michael, I was just looking through my clothes in your wardrobe for something to wear tomorrow and I notice there's a dark brown suit hanging there and a trilby hat on the shelf. What's that all about? I didn't even know you owned a suit, let alone a hat!'

Michael pulled his attention away from the television and looked at his wife with a vague expression.

'Oh, that, I thought I told you. A few months ago, the owners decided on a regular weekly breakfast meeting at that posh hotel down the road, you know the one. Anyway, I needed to look the 'executive' part so I bought the suit and hat. Are you sure I didn't tell you? I'm certain I did. We meet every Wednesday morning and then I catch the bus and head on into work.'

Ruth just sat there, staring, lost for words yet needing to respond to Michael's explanation. All she could think of was, for the past few months she'd been dreaming and fantasising about her own husband!

Michael's voice broke into her thoughts. 'Oh, yes, I meant to say earlier. The Wednesday meeting is off tomorrow, not sure why, so I decided to take the day off. Would you be awfully disappointed if you missed your retail therapy? Perhaps we might have that day out we've talked about for so long, see the Tower of London; then perhaps dinner and a theatre show after. We could do with spending some quality time together.'

'That would be lovely,' answered Ruth. 'How about turning off the TV and locking up the house? After all, you know how that movie ends. Let's have an early night; we haven't done that in a long time either. And maybe an adventure or two, before tomorrow?' she said, with a twinkle in her eye.

And as they climbed the stairs together, it came back to Ruth where she had smelled the fragrance on the suit and she remembered the dream of a few months back – a skiff, a gently flowing river, the warm sun on her face and the lovely aroma that tantalised her nostrils as she drifted along.

Hot Rocks

Ruth switched off the hall light, closed their bedroom door and turned – and for the first time in ages she smiled as she approached the bed, her husband sitting there with his arms open wide, waiting for her.

Muddy Boots

Denise Delaney

'Aquamarine ?'

'a.q.u.a.m.a.r.i.n.e. Encased, the sea gently rises and falls in shades of blue and green. Aquamarine.'

I watch Dad with his girls, 30 still to go. He knows them all by name. It's noisy in the yard with cows mooing and shoving, a chaotic counterpoint to the background roar of the milking machines and the vacuum cups busily sucking and slurping away.

'Somnambulist?'

's.o.m.n.a.m.b.u.l.i.s.t. Dreaming, I wander the farm. Somnambulist.'

Dad's seat is a slice through a tree, and years of sitting and washing leave it with a dark shiny top and woodgrains separating at the bottom. He's wearing the usual tatty straw hat that once a year is decked with a rising sun badge, a white singlet (the checked flannelette shirt is abandoned and flung over the split rail fence), heavy drill khaki trousers and his big black wellingtons that squeak with every step.

'Alliteration on ... b.'

'a.l.l.i.t.e.r.a.t.i.o.n. Beautiful brown-eyed bovines, big, broad and buxom, bellowing. Alliteration.'

He opens the gate and Old Daisy walks through. Closes it and I'm off down the yard to bring up the next cow. I choose Flossie, the only roan in a herd of tall, deep-red, Australian Illawarra Shorthorns, who plays games, heading towards the bales then suddenly veering away. I enjoy the chase, sloshing through the deep mud, squishing it between my toes and splashing it up my legs.

'Arcane?'

'a.r.c.a.n.e. Ah Cain, said God. Whatdidya do that for? No secrets from God. Arcane.'

Betty, with no encouragement from me, wanders up and enters the empty stall; Dad puts the leg-rope on, washes her udder then, squeezing each teat in turn, gets the milk to flow, puts on the cups and moves to the next cow.

The routine of cows and questions continues. The mud dries on my legs and every hop or slip creates cracks in the once-solid brown. A sudden memory of the patterns made on the mudflats in last year's drought emerges and fades away. Flossie is last in and last out, as always, then we (with Dad doing most of the work) clean up and head to the house for dinner.

I detour by the rusty, corrugated-iron tank to wash off my muddy boots, watching them gurgle away in brown spirals down the cement drain. Bright red flashes of chipped and pitted toenail polish appear, and I inspect a tender spot on my sole.

Hot Rocks

I head inside, leaving a trail of damp footprints on the wooden veranda, then the linoleum floor, wondering how I'll go in the spelling and comprehension tests; and how did cousin Bill transform his feet into such tough leather that even thistles are repelled; and then there's Flossie – why does she always go last? Her choice, the herd's choice, or just chance perpetuated and ritualised? Big issues to think about after milking time.

Jupiter Station

Craig Slobin

Captain Toni gave a little jump as the radio com crackled to life in her ear. Who could blame her? It was eerie enough out here in deep space without having to investigate a ghost station. Jupiter Station was orbiting the moon Europa and all contact had been lost two months ago. It irked her having to sit here alone on the rescue ship Bounty, while her three crewmen searched it. It was one of the largest stations too, so it was taking a long time to accomplish the task. A long time for her to fret and get nervous, but at least somebody was finally calling in. She hated space, especially when there was only silence and her own anxious thoughts. Silence in deep space caused those thoughts to make her feel very small and vulnerable.

'Captain ... they're all accounted for,' crackled Sergeant Tobias's voice.

She waited for more information. None was forthcoming, so she clicked the intercom on her headset as she tapped the fuzzy screen on the console before her.

'And?' she asked impatiently, giving the screen a solid slap. Finally, she could see Tobias's face in his helmet, over there in the dark.

He stared back from the monitor, looking pale. 'And the rest are all dead, Captain. Just like the young woman said.' She frowned at that: the young woman, the apparent sole survivor. Well, there wasn't anything 'apparent' about it now, was there? All dead, all but one; this was a big station, too. Their debriefing informed them there were ten people residing here. Military and civilians both, or *had* lived here, she supposed.

What in the world has happened?

Of course, they weren't in the world, were they, or on it? They were stuck out here in lonely space and she felt even more alone now she knew for certain Jupiter Station was empty; empty of the living at any rate.

'Shit!' she cursed, more in frustration than in anger or grief. After all, she didn't know any of these people, these corpses. 'Can she speak yet?'

The sergeant's helmet jiggled as he shrugged, his brown eyes glancing to the left. 'Yes and no.'

What kind of answer is that?

'Can she tell us what happened or not, Sergeant?' she replied crisply, as the screen went fuzzy again. Another slap and Tobias came back into focus.

'No, Captain,' was his troubled reply. 'We can't get much out of her at all. She keeps muttering about her medication. Apparently one of her friends over here hid it from her as a joke.'

Toni sighed and rubbed her face. 'Where's Michael?'

'I'm here, Captain.' The corporal and ship's medic must have clicked his camera panel because the screen changed vantage and she found herself staring at the survivor. The young lady looked a mess, she was sitting on the metal floor, rocking back and forth and muttering away to herself with big, scared eyes.

'Do you know what kind of meds she was on?' she asked, eyes glued to the young lady before whom the corporal squatted. 'Can we give her something?'

'Already have, Captain,' he replied as his metal glove clasped the woman's shoulder. 'By the look of her I reckon she suffers acute anxiety. Like most of us out here. And she hasn't had her meds for two months.' Toni wasn't alone with her desolate feeling in space. Most space workers, if not all, needed relaxants to get through any day; civilians like these marine biologists even more so, she presumed.

'I've given her three doses of Valium,' Michael continued as they watched the woman. She could be no more than eighteen, probably out here for her last year of study and practical. Well, more fool her, because there was nothing practical about space work. This station was orbiting Europa for a very important reason and no doubt the girl's mind had been filled with discovering life out here, or down there on one of the moons of Jupiter.

'All right, well, bring her over and tuck her in, Michael. That's enough Valium to even put me to sleep,' she said with an anxious rub to her face. The man nodded as her screen flickered to yet another vantage, this one even darker, aside from a solitary torch beam.

Hot Rocks

'Captain! Captain!' it was Shay's excited voice in her ear and the private's beaming face in the shadowy helmet. 'You gotta see this!'

Toni sighed; trust Private Shay to be wearing a grin in a station full of dead people, a metal tomb orbiting a distant moon. 'See what, Private?' she asked.

'They did it, Toni!' The youngest member of her crew was brimming with excitement, hardly the sombreness she should be conducting her search with. It was downright disrespectful.

'Shay!' she scolded her. 'People have died. Behave yourself or I'll put a mark in your record!'

'Screw that!' The pretty woman's blue eyes were agog in her visor. 'Look! Look, Toni!'

The view on the screen flickered again as the private pressed a button and she could now see the darkened room. It was a laboratory. At first she didn't know what she was supposed to be looking at until Shay's torch lit up a water tank on a desktop.

'Holy shit!' she exclaimed in complete shock.

Could it be? ... It has to be ...

She doubted very much these scientists would have brought it with them from earth. She didn't think they could have anyway; surely it would have died on the long journey. Besides, none of the space stations sprinkled around the solar system was permitted any life-forms from home; that would risk contamination. Several times over the past few years newfound life had been proclaimed to the people of earth only to be proved false. Each and every time the microscopic life-forms had turned out to be from earth, tiny microbes that had stowed away in or on a spaceship.

The United Nations was extremely strict with all protocols now. The last thing the leaders of the world needed was more false celebrations, not to mention the different religions' condemnation and scoffing when the new life was proven false. Every time that happened, the governments of the world gave less funding to the search for extra-terrestrial life. After five years of fruitless searching, more and more people were turning back to religion and away from science.

'Holy shit!' she repeated, eyes as wide as the private's now. At first she wasn't sure exactly what she was looking at, even with Shay's beam of light, until her mind registered what it was. It made sense, she guessed, or at least it was remotely possible. After all, Jupiter Station was so big and had so many marine biologists for a very good reason. The moon Europa whizzing by beneath them was an ice satellite, and that thick ice crust had a gigantic ocean beneath that covered the entire moon.

'Damn, Toni,' crackled the private's voice as she got even closer to the tank. 'Check it out.' Shay tapped the glass and the jellyfish within jerked away from the clink of metal glove on glass. 'And watch this,' she continued. Suddenly her torch went out. 'It's bioluminescent!' As soon as the light disappeared, Toni had to blink at the screen as the jellyfish burst into a dazzling display of glowing rainbow colours.

Wow!

'We found life, Captain!' exclaimed Shay. 'We fucking found life!'

As exciting as this was, it wasn't their mission to find life. It was all of those poor dead people's missions and thinking of that made her calm down and return to the task at hand.

'All right, Private,' she said. 'Find something to put it in, and bring it back over. Then you can return to the station and start retrieving the bodies.' She didn't await a response and this time it was she who changed the camera, back to the sergeant. 'Tobias,' was her only greeting. 'Why is everybody dead?' Despite discovering the jellyfish, something irked her still. What had happened here to kill so many scientists? 'What have you worked out?'

The sergeant sat down in the command centre of the station and began tapping away at the keyboard as he spoke through the com. 'Well, they're all over the place, but each death actually looks accidental. Three were in their quarters and appear to have vented the air out; two were spacewalking and seem to have locked themselves out. They also ran out of air. I think you can see them.'

She nodded, even though he was watching his own computer screen. She also glanced up at the two immobile, floating spacesuits tethered to the top of the station and gave a shudder as that sense of dread and loneliness returned. She heard Corporal Michael enter the ship behind her through the airlock. She also heard the air vent a second time as Private Shay returned after him, supposedly with the alien jellyfish.

'Two more choked on their rations in the mess,' continued Tobias calmly. 'Or so Michael says. We found one drowned in her bathtub and the last looks like a suicide. He hanged himself in the lab Shay was in. Michael said he was the first to go.'

Any elation at finding an alien ebbed away from her. It was a tragic event, many tragic events. No wonder the lone survivor was having an episode, especially since she couldn't find her meds. Toni couldn't survive out here without her daily Valium, let alone being trapped all alone surrounded by the corpses of her colleagues and friends.

The poor, poor girl.

Still, something didn't feel right and her mind flashed back to the jellyfish.

No, that's just silly, absolutely crazy, how could a jellyfish in a tank kill all those people?

'All right ...' she said, as she thought. 'Send all their logs over then, Sergeant,' she commanded. 'And then you and Shay can bring the bodies over. And make it quick, huh? This place gives me the heebee-jeebees. Let's get the fuck out of here.'

'You won't have to tell me twice, Captain,' he crackled in agreement.

Toni gave her deepest sigh yet as the cockpit door behind her opened, and she spoke without turning her head from the view screen. 'How is the poor girl, Michael?' There was only silence. The quiet was so absolute it gave her a shiver again. 'Well, answer me, goddammit it! I'm spooked enough as it is!'

Still nothing. Just the oppressive and overwhelming silence punctuated by very faint breathing, causing her to spin around in her pilot chair with a fright, only to chuckle with relief when she found the young woman standing there.

'Hello, honey,' she greeted her. The girl only stared at her with vacant eyes. That was when she noticed the blood-covered scissors in her hand, and it wasn't old, dried blood either; it was fresh and dripping off the blades to splatter on the metal floor of the cockpit.

Captain Toni drew in a huge breath, ready to scream, just as she heard Sergeant Tobias's voice crackle over the com. 'Hey, I think I found the young woman's medication.' His voice changed slightly as he read the label. 'Ah ... they're anti-psychotic tablets.'

Of course, in space nobody can hear you scream.

Postcard from Karumba

Diane Jensen

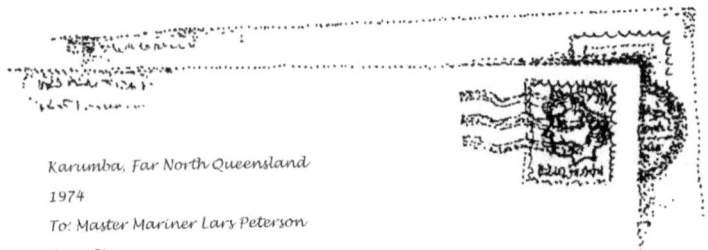

Karumba, Far North Queensland

1974

To: Master Mariner Lars Peterson

Dear Sir,

Since I returned to the trawlers from your classes in Cairns, the prawn season has been full on. Now that I have my Masters Ticket from your course, I am appreciating more respect and my wages are higher (sorry re behaviour in class sometimes!) Just thought you may like this little verse, comprising the names of all the types of prawns we catch! Not to mention the Moreton Bay Bugs you so enjoy:

> In our trawlers, we ENDEAVOUR to KING the prawn seasons and
> catch large SCHOOLS. However, the stripey TIGERS have to be our
> main catch at night when the BANANAS skid away by day. Then
> our fearless LEADER will CORAL us together and we'll BUGGer off
> to new fishing grounds!

Your recalcitrant sole female student,

Wendy.

A Slice of Life in Canberra

Margaret Drury

We were living in Canberra and grew apricots between us and the house of Pietro and Roberta, our neighbours. The trees produced abundantly and we made many delicious products from them but also were able to give them away to neighbours both sides and down the lane. We were lucky enough to have a wall on the warm side of the house where they grew happily.

Pietro and Roberta owned two fierce Alsatian dogs which didn't like anyone except their family members. They would snarl at us if we met them while going for a walk. Pietro had been a farmer in South Africa before the whites were kicked out. Roberta had two sons, Julius and Jonno, both at the best private school for boys in Canberra. We once saw Jonno kicking Zuba, one of the Alsatians, to make him obey. From then on, Zuba became vicious. The other, a female, was more docile. The boys' sister Rita played the piano and harpsichord. Later, when all the children were off their hands, Pietro and Roberta bought a property down the coast near Bega where the dogs could roam as they pleased.

Rita's musical abilities took her all over Australia with the Woden Valley choir. She was a much sought-after accompanist and we felt privileged to listen to her practising, and to attend with her, when she played on stage at the School of Music. Later, she was to have a wedding which was unusually eventful and almost disastrous. I'll come to that.

Meanwhile, across the road, were two little Chihuahuas belonging to Elsie and Barry. Although normally kept well away from Pietro's Alsatians, they were unfortunately mistaken for rats by the bigger dogs. This ended badly!

Our mostly-peaceful lives in Canberra were quickly shattered by the advent of "the big fires". They began on a day of extreme heat and high winds. Although the suburb where we lived was away from the fire front, a freak incident occurred. An electric wire fell onto a hedge of shrubs which caught fire, throwing a sudden fireball. A powerful gust of wind sent the fireball across the roads. It hit a woodpile beside a house only four doors down from us. The logs caught fire and that house plus the one next door to it were consumed by raging fire. If it hadn't been for the water bombing planes spraying over us continually, who knows how much worse it could have been? No lives were lost in our part of Canberra but in the south, many more houses were lost and five people died.

The wedding of Pietro's daughter Rita, was on this day of fires. A coach and two horses were hired to take the bride to and from the church. The trouble was, Pietro couldn't give his daughter away. Her brother Julius had to do that. Pietro was up on the roof of his house, with a long hose pouring water everywhere so his ancient Italian mother – being very distressed – would feel safe. However, Pietro eventually did get to the reception hall on his motorbike in time to make his speech.

Cousin Too

Terry Dunkley

I was born in Sydney and spent the first four years of my childhood there. Dad was a motor mechanic and a pretty good one at that, but he always longed for something else in his life. He used to recount the 'flower power' days and wished he'd been old enough to be part of that movement, to go to San Francisco with flowers in his hair and spread love around and perhaps to live in a commune.

These were some of his ideals, whereas his two brothers were the opposite, calling him a 'bloody poofter' for thinking like that.

By the time I was four, Dad had persuaded Mum to move away from the city to a more rural area, perhaps a small town up north. He would be able to get a job. The money would not be the same, but neither would the living costs. Four years after that, we were living in North Queensland and loving it. Dad put a deposit on ten acres of cleared rainforest. The loggers had been through and left very little, but the ground was rich and fertile. It was exactly what Dad wanted, to be on the road to self sufficiency or as close to it as possible.

There was still work for him in town, and Mum did a bit of part-time nursing at the old people's home, but any disposable income went into the property. We planted every conceivable tropical fruit tree: lychee, rambutan, soursop, white supote, breadfruit and so many other species. The lychee was one of the fastest growing and didn't take long to start bearing fruit. We got little off it at first because the parrots used to eat most of them, and at night we could hear the fruit bats squabbling in that tree. A possum even had a nest up there next to a food source, but as the tree grew more prolific there was more fruit left for us.

We were happier than we ever thought possible in these beautiful surroundings. There was a special joy in going outside and picking our own breakfast, and the air was so clean and unpolluted, except for the fragrance of flowering trees.

When I was sixteen, one of my cousins came to stay with us for two weeks. He had never been outside of Sydney and I just couldn't wait to meet him and to show him all the beautiful trees and shrubs and to take him into the wondrous rainforest. I'd been to Sydney once on a school trip and found it too noisy, fast and dusty and had been glad of the experience, but more glad to get home. Now I could show my cousin why.

The train slowly came to a halt. People on the platform looked anxiously at the passengers, and the passengers looked out anxiously at those on the platform, eager to recognise their contacts. Finally, Dad spotted my cousin. Roy was close to my age but a casual observer would not know we were related. We were the same height but he had a slight build, a sickly pallor and a slumping of the shoulders. He was mopping his forehead with a large white handkerchief,

'Too hot!' He said as his first greeting. He later became known as Cousin Too, as everything was too hot, too wet, too quiet or too boring. On the third day of his visit, I took him for a walk in the wondrous rainforest to where a little creek ran down past a waterfall and through a peaty bed. I lay down on the mossy bank, scooped up a handful of the clear water and drank it. Filtered by nature, it was pure and cool.

'Don't drink that!' Too shouted, 'It's full of bacteria.'

'Try it,' I replied. 'That is the sweetest water you will ever taste.'

'No way,' he said. 'I only drink water from a tap because that's where clean water comes from.' I felt sad for him, but also angered by his manner and his ignorance, more so because he did not want to see or learn anything. To him, milk would always come from the corner store.

'What's that?' he said, fearfully pointing to a black thing wriggling on his white leg.

'It's a leech,' I replied. 'Keep still and I'll get it off.' He let out a scream and dashed away down the path along which we had come. Eventually I caught up with him and brought him down with a rugby tackle, then held his screaming, kicking form as I pulled off the leech – and it was a lot bigger by this time.

That evening he phoned his father. 'Dad, I've got to come home tomorrow. There are too many awful things around here that sting, bite and suck blood.'

Next day Cousin Too was on the train heading south. That one little leech had turned out to be a godsend.

630 minutes

Denise Delaney

It's 9.30 p.m., and the television is switched off. It has been another bad news week, with floods, earthquakes, tsunamis and now the threat of nuclear annihilation. I wonder why the media have determined that we must follow, as it happens, the agonisingly destructive paths the waves have taken, watching mankind's unbreakable concrete structures being easily breached and focusing on the now-deathly silence where once-bustling communities disappeared into the wall of mud. I also wonder what Oriental nations feel about the West's voyeuristic press, wallowing in the rising tide of the dead and missing.

Hubris ... hmmm.

Big issues when the small ones are more than enough for me.

The preparations for bedtime begin: toileting, cleaning false teeth, assembling the night's needs in the bathroom, and administering the tablets for the evening. I take Mum to her room and make a nest of blankets, sheets and pillows. She tells me she'll see me at 2.30. I know that number is on her wish list, which sometimes comes true, but is more often on the optimistic side. The bedside lamp is off, and I head back to my lounge room for some reading, drawing and mulling over the day's events. This is when I typically work on cartoons, transforming the day's irritations, the good, the bad and the downright silly, into humour (which helps explain the underlying blackness in them). I love this time of night when the whole earth seems to be asleep and a comforting darkness prevails. At 11.00 p.m., my rituals for self-preservation complete, I head to bed.

I wake at 12.30, listening to the house breathe around me. I know the noises the house makes, the creaks and contractions of the metal roof, the regular low thumping of the hot water heat-pump, the rattle of my now-ageing refrigerator, the bellyflop slap of frogs on windows and an awareness of sharp feline claws touching the door, wanting out. This time it is soft nasally in-breaths followed by the flapping of cheeks, then another and another. I shake off the dream I was inhabiting, trying to delete the image of a crocodile living on my veranda (it's a sweet crocodile, a kind, soft and fluffy crocodile, a familiar and regular visitor in my dreams that is totally unlike the cold-blooded, snapping real ones, and it doesn't create fear, but it is still a crocodile), and focus on the monitor beside my bed.

The crocodile ... harbinger of death and of rebirth ... the dark ogre deeply embedded in the collective unconscious, in our souls, a legacy from our fearful African ancestors.

I wonder what invaded my sleep, then recognise the familiar shuffling in bed as Mum rolls over, the creaking of the wooden slats under her mattress and the slight crunching noise made by freshly starched and ironed sheets being thrown off. I hear her light wheezing as she sits upright, then the calling of my name. I'm quickly out of bed, throw an elastic-waisted black-and-white spotted skirt over my shoulders and pull it down until it covers from my boobs to my knees, shove my feet into sandals and head to her room to gauge and assuage her needs. I'm sure it will be the usual.

By 12.50, ablutions are complete, the next round of tablets is taken and Mum is tucked back into her bed. I whisper 'sweet dreams', pat her gently on the hip, switch off lights and head to my room, shedding the skirt where habit makes me drape it on my bedpost, within easy reach in the dark and leaving shoes where my feet naturally touch the floor.

The light is out, my soul at rest.
A beckoning finger draws me to sleep,
to the uncontrolled deep of dreams and nightmares.
The finger wags, a fist clenches.
The healing torpor, the embracing arms of Morpheus
are no longer mine to command.

Its 2.10 and I'm still awake. I haven't solved any of the world's problems, although my thinking is at its clearest (if I could only remember the universal panaceas I thought up in the cold light of the day) and to compound things, I now have twitchy legs. Dancing legs I could cope with (aggh ... please, not in my bed), but the uncontrollable urge to squirm and jerk dominates my thoughts. (I remember the old exercise where students were told *not* to think of a bear, in no circumstances to allow even a passing thought of a bear to cross their minds and of course, when asked five minutes later what they were thinking at that instant, they replied: koalas, 'if you go down to the woods today you're sure of a big surprise', 'grizzlies', 'there's a bear in there', pandas and polars.) I haven't decided which comes first but, when I go to bed determined tonight there will be no twitching, then invariably that is the night they 'trip the light fantastic'. If that thought does not enter my mind then I quietly drift away. Now for my big question: Do I think the forbidden thoughts because my subconscious has already prophesied there is a twitch a'coming, or is it the articulation of that thought that generates the jerk and squirm? Chicken or egg? Egg or chicken?

At 2.25, thinking 'Thank heavens I'm bipedal' (with the thought mulling around in the back of my mind that my arms never seem to have this twitch) I get out of bed, walk around stretching, then massaging my legs, rubbing oil into muscles, wonder if magnesium really works and is it too late to try now? I do some knee bends and leg raises then return to bed and, sometime soon after, I drift away.

Legs, walking, taking me to my friends, to my social connections, to my family ... breaking down separation and isolation ... Legs, linking me with others, helping to maintain the ties that bind me to my society. Legs, symbols of movement, of life.

4.15 a.m. The house again breathes in my ears. I drag myself out of sleep and when I hear my name, I am back on duty. I'm walking by rote, avoiding doorways, lounge chairs and a supine cat lying in the middle of the hall. I am trying not to fully open my eyes, not to wake totally but when the commode chair swivels and bangs into the loo, I belatedly jam on the brakes. I have to focus. Toileting complete, and with Mum back in bed, I head to mine, fall in and am instantly asleep.

I wake suddenly to the sound of my name. I mumble 'coming' and the voice replies 'about time, and so is Christmas'. I roll out of bed, listen hyper-vigilantly, but hear nothing more sinister than quiet breathing. I throw on my modesty skirt and make my way to the bedroom door. All is quiet within. I open the toilet door a sliver, shedding light into the bedroom. Mum is sound asleep, curled up like a baby; one hand cups her face, the other a small fist on her chest. The pillow is plumped around her neck and her legs are bent in a foetal position. I slink back to bed cursing my brain for dreaming this up. This had to be a dream as Mum has been gracious, thankful and kind since she moved in with me (although there was a time in the past where 'Christmas' was always coming). I sleep.

At 7.15, the morning sunlight makes its appearance through my bedroom doors. It's almost overwhelmingly bright, then becomes muted as the mist rises up through the valley. The insect screens collect moisture in the metal grids that looks like dew droplets on a mechanical spider's web. The kookaburras have been, laughing the dawn a welcome, and now the butcherbirds bring me their joyful, melodious songs, reminding me I should be feeding them the previous day's leftovers, otherwise they'll implement their underlying threat of appeasing their hunger on the fairy wrens or honeyeaters. I don't have a formal agreement with them, just a verbal harangue to leave the wee ones alone, and a promise to feed them if they do.

I lie in bed, absorbing the serenity of Alaskan Jade walls, translucent white curtains moving gently in the updraught, the reflections of Buddha's eighteen disciples in an oak antique, round-mirrored dressing table, and vibrant splashes of colour in pots, decorative plates and dried flowers. I love my valley view. I savour this peaceful time, this little window of freedom, till 8.00 when the daily rituals of being a carer really begin.

Valleys ... gullies meet, join to form a valley, the feminine eternal opens, receiving the waters streaming down its sides, filling the hollows and voids bringing fertility, fecundity, verdancy ... valleys ... pathways, passages for journeys of the spirit, giving the soul the space to soar then rest in safety ... valleys ... open and enclosed ... receptacles for celestial influences from the sun, the moon, the stars and the fruitful hands of Gaia.

Hot Rocks

Far, far away I hear the jingling of tiny bells.
An invitation appears.
Come to the gate.
Step over the threshold into the great adventure beyond.
Gates open ... Come now.
I cannot.
Gates close.
Locked.
Here ... then ... Gone.

Postcard from Edinburgh

Craig Slobin

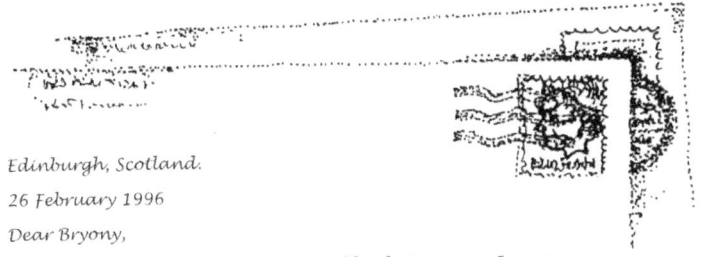

Edinburgh, Scotland.

26 February 1996

Dear Bryony,

I'm giving up. It's been 13 knockbacks in a row. I mean, what was I thinking? Now all those people will think I'm an idiot, an utter novice. Worse, they'll think me childish. Oh, god! I even made words up! Made them up, Bryony! Ooh, this word sounds funny, why don't I use it instead of a real one! I'll be a laughing stock. What am I saying? I already am a laughing stock! I'll never be able to leave my house again, not ever! Now, don't you be writing back telling me I'm good at what I do, because I'm crap at it. And don't you tell me how much you love the book either. No more lies, Bryony. I'm giving up and that's that. Anyway, I've got one more knockback letter to open; after that I'm done with writing forever.

Yours truly,

Joanne K. Rowling

Family Dreams

Robin Hammond

It is 1962 and Mum has pinned all her hopes on me. I am to be the first person in the family – male or female – to attend university. My mother was born in 1915 to parents who believed in higher education for women and her own mother had held the same hopes for her. Mum had a 'Genius' IQ, so my Nanna's ambitions were well-founded. In those days, very few girls carried on past their third year of high school. Mum was one of only two in a class of 32 boys to reach the Leaving Certificate.

Alas, the boys were more interesting to Mum than the study of Latin. Hormones and a naturally-flighty disposition got in the way and sank my Nanna's dreams of having a Nobel Laureate in the family. Although Mum passed her Leaving Certificate, her results were underwhelming. She went on to a career in secretarial work.

I tell you this story because, oh dear, history seems to be repeating itself. Although I closet myself in my room each night, I'm more interested in writing notes to boys, telephoning friends, sneaking out to meet up when we should be studying, and concentrating on my latest ambition: to smoke an entire packet of Craven A cigarettes in one day.

Hot Rocks

Exam time for the Leaving Certificate looms and, at the last minute, I decide on an unconventional method of cramming. I have no real idea how to 'study' but do have a photographic memory, so I decide to memorise the relevant chapters of the textbooks for each subject. I now look back and realise how ridiculous this was. I walk into the exam rooms every day with my head full of memorised text which I then attempt to apply to the various questions. This is fine for subjects like French and Latin but useless for History, Geography, Physics and others that require a degree of analysis and original thought.

My results, when they come, are almost a replica of Mum's. I pass but, according to the requirements of the day, those who cannot afford to pay for tertiary education must perform exceptionally well in the Leaving Certificate to qualify for a Commonwealth Scholarship. In 1962, university education is almost solely reserved for the wealthy.

Of course I am upset. I had daydreamed of lolling on sunlit lawns at the foot of ivy-clad sandstone walls, surrounded by attentive, debonair and very brainy suitors. My ambition to study at university disappears down the drain.

Having first vented her disappointment, Mum drags a very unwilling me along to secretarial college. 'You'll always get a job with shorthand/typing,' she says. She knows this from experience.

Hot Rocks

I hate the college, the teachers, my classmates and the course but instead of flunking out, I decide to use my brain for a change and rush through the 48-week course in eight weeks whereupon I leave, joyfully waving my certificate. This proves to me what I could have done if I had buckled down to my school studies. I push that thought aside and set out to find a job. Mum, of course, is right. I get work whenever and wherever I want it and am sought after because I have a bit of intelligence and also know how to spell and punctuate.

Years pass. I marry and travel around Australia, settling in Cairns for a few years, where I produce two sons. But always, in the back of my mind is that niggle of regret for that lost opportunity. My dear mother has never breathed a word of reproach since the exam debacle.

We are still living in Cairns when, on 1 January 1974, Prime Minister Gough Whitlam introduces free tertiary education for all. What's more, the University of New England in Armidale establishes itself as a leading provider of distance education and offers enrolment to mature-age students. The only criterion is the ability to express oneself with intelligence in a 300-word essay. This I can do, and with glee I grab this gift with both hands. I become a fully-fledged university student and over the next 20 years immerse myself successfully in the academic world. I love it.

Hot Rocks

But there is a sad coda to this story. My poor mother is slowly developing frontal-lobe dementia. When I announce that I've at last enrolled at university, she looks at me with total lack of interest: 'That's nice,' she says and returns to staring out the window at my children playing in the sandpit. I often kick myself for being such a silly teenager and not giving my dearly-loved mother the pleasure of seeing her dreams fulfilled.

Strangled Love

Diane Jensen

Live with me

And I

Will show you how

That

In time

We will

Destroy each other.

Outback Dunny

Margaret Drury

Tinkle, tinkle, twinkle, twinkle

When I'm in the outside dunny

'I can see the twinkle of a star

Through the crack on a fine night

Or maybe the moon

Peeping in at me on my throne

It's a good job there isn't

Really a Man in the Moon

To see me in my nightie going

Tinkle tinkle.

A Lucky Escape

Lucy Powter

Captain Lewis studied the weather and found it was predicted to be a good, gentle evening. He wanted the crew of his fishing trawler to have another go at filling the remaining space in the freezers.

Apart from Captain Lewis, the crew was made up of three others: Tom was a large man with sun-damaged skin, and hirsute body and limbs covered in tattoos; Bill was an elderly man, and a mate of Captain Lewis's father. Having been around boats all his life, he had skills in trawler repairs and fishing; Fred was in his teens, and the youngest crew member. He suffered sea sickness and was thought by the others to be a bit of an idiot. He tried hard but always seemed to do something wrong. Captain Lewis had a lot of empathy for Fred, remembering how clumsy and seasick he had been when he was Fred's age. But he had recovered, worked hard and now owned his trawler. He felt Fred would succeed too.

The winch was groaning as it hauled in the net full of thrashing fish. Tom called out over the noise, 'Open the neck!' as he grabbed the swinging net to steady it.

Fred, fumbling around on the wet deck, managed to grab the slippery rope at the opening and yelled, 'Got it!' He, and the captain, who had come to help as he always did, pulled hard on the rope and the net spilled its writhing contents into the huge collection trays on the deck.

'Let's sort them out,' said the captain to Tom and Fred. 'Bill, turn the winch off.' It was a good haul. The crew sorted, packed the fish by size into boxes, then into the freezer. The rest was thrown back.

Everything appeared to be going well until Fred, still weak from sea sickness, and carrying one of the boxes for the freezer, slipped on the slimy deck. The box went flying and fish landed everywhere. Fred was prostrate on the deck. The crew began to laugh and then froze, when suddenly a wave washed onto the deck and Fred was swept towards the gunnels. His body slipped under the lower gunnel rail and was half into the ocean.

'Bloody hell!' shouted Captain Lewis. 'Grab him!' First to act, he latched onto Fred's ankles, just in time to stop another wash of wave sweeping Fred further over. The other men scrambled to help, pulling a terrified, helpless Fred to safety. They wedged the shivering and shaking Fred into a corner of the deck and all took a deep breath of relief.

Leaving Fred safe to recover from his ordeal, and with the catch all processed and in the freezers, the crew washed down the deck and made ready, while the captain headed back to port. He was satisfied the fish co-op would buy his haul for a good price, and very happy he'd not lost Fred over the side! He couldn't help smiling as he steered to home.

As for Fred – he just wanted to be back on land to tell his story of near-death at sea.

Removalling

Christopher Hammond

I'm a Removalist; that's me job and I love it with a passion. Got a great team of blokes who never lets me down. This last job, though, tested us proper. I think Kingy's gone blind, Davo lost a finger and Big Mick still hasn't stopped spewing; but it's done. Towards the end, we was sick to bloody death of it but we had to finish, no matter what. I wrote up the worksheets every day, so I think I got it right. This is how it went down.

DAY ONE

We get to the house early. Weather's fine; it's a beaut day for removalling a house. Davo's been out to do the quote and says it's an easy one. Old Mabel's just about finished the packing, so it'll be in and out in a day or two. That's what I was thinkin' anyway; then Mabel comes stormin' out.

'I don't know what bloody dickhead done the quote but there's nothin' I can do about that vat in the cellar. I done the wine but jesus, fellas, what the fuck was I supposed to do with all that bloody rum?'

'Davo,' I says, 'what's Mabel talkin' about?'

'Jeez, Boss, I dunno. I never seen no cellar.'

Hot Rocks

How the hell could Davo miss an entire bloody wine cellar? Then I realise. I know the sheila what owns the place and she's a stunner. Bloody Davo, thinkin' with his dick as usual, couldn't see past her cleavage when he was doin' the quote. Looks like I'm goin' to have to revise it. Talk about embarrassin'.

'Sorry Mabel,' I say. 'We'll check it out and you can take off home, darlin'.'

'Sendin' a dickhead to do a woman's work, that was,' says Mabel, and I can't help but agree.

'Okay, file out fellas,' I say, motioning them to go where Mabel's pointed out the cellar.

So, sittin' in the middle of the cellar is a massive vat of rum. The bloody thing must be four feet high and about as round. We can see the brand name in big yellow letters on the side: 'Corpus Delicto'.

'Well shit, eh?' says Kingy. That much rum would kill ya alright.' He's walking around kicking it. 'About a quarter full, Boss, no way we're movin' it. Gonna have to drain it in here. The whole fucken place would go up if ya lit a fag within a hundred metres. Gonna have to drink it Boss, no other way.'

There are other ways, plenty of them, but we all likes our rum so I don't pull rank on him. 'Okay boys, listen up. The rest of today is for draining the vat.' I see their eyes light up. 'Make sure you're sober enough to cook, Davo.'

Davo nods. He's only a young bloke but he learned him some cheffin' in Long Bay. He cooks on the big jobs.

I didn't see Big Mick leave but now he's back. 'Cups.' He's rooted around in the packing and found four pint glasses and he passes them around.

'I guess our illustrious leader should do the honours,' says Kingy. So I steps up to the tap and pours meself a pint of rum. The others follow and then wait for me.

'To the art of removalling boys. 'Up yer bum!'

'Up yer bum!' they all chorus and we take a pull. It's strong. Kinda funny-tasting but good, real good. We make our camp in the cellar and that's about us for the day. We sits about drinking.

When it gets dark, we send Davo upstairs to cook. Then it happens.

'AAARGH! Fuck!' yells Davo and we stumble upstairs into the kitchen and there's blood everywhere. Davo stands in the centre of the kitchen, looking down at his hand. 'I'm sorry, Boss, I messed up,' says Davo. 'It's not good Boss, it's real bad.' I move around so I can see Davo's hand. 'I was tryin' to open the tomato sauce with me knife, Boss but I messed up.' I can see his hand now and it's all blood. 'It's gone, Boss, totally gone.' There's the wreckage of a tomato sauce bottle in his hand. What I thought was blood everywhere was actually the sauce. 'The whole bottle, Boss, all gone.' Davo looks like he's gonna cry.

'Okay, boys. Chin up,' I says, tryin' to lighten the mood. 'We're just gonna have to eat without tomato sauce for a coupla days.' But the room is silent.

We don't even try to eat dinner and little Davo can't stop crying. I can tell this removal's gonna test us.

DAY TWO

The day starts quiet. We're hungover something fierce and eating last night's dinner, heated up on the old camp stove. Davo takes his out on the porch. He's doin' a Garbo and that's fine, we don't push him. When he's back in the kitchen and we're all together, I try to motivate them.

'Okay, lads, rocky start, but let's get movin' on it. Mick and Davo downstairs, Kingy can help me with the house and supervise the drinkin' –not too much, Kingy, we gotta be able to walk straight and work straight. Removalists, roll out!'

The day goes pretty smooth until three in the arvo. The lads are havin' smoko while I do the logs, then I hear Kingy.

'Boss, come down here!' He's been in the cellar, trying to calculate how many litres of rum we've got left. I hop it down. 'Okay, Boss, we've each had about two litres today, that's why we're all pretty wobbly. And the tap on the keg is getting blocked by somethin' rattling around in there. But get a loada this: I found a bloody rabbit trap down here. Mabel left a note on it for us.' The note was pretty typical:

Hot Rocks

If youse bloody dickheads think I'm gonna pack up a loaded bloody rabit trap you've got another think coming. I rekon that young bloke davo wot thinks with his dick, make him pick the dam thing up.

This is an annoyance.

'Davo! Get your bloody arse down here!' Davo come stumblin' down the stairs; he's so slaughtered, he misses the last three and comes cannoning into Kingy, both of 'em ending up on the floor.

'Oh, shit. Sorry Kingy. Someone moved the steps there, mate.'

'S'okay Davo, I think we've all got our wobbly boots on this arvo.'

'Holy shit, Boss! Look at this!' says Davo. 'It's a bloody bear trap. I seen one of them in a video game once. This bloke set it off like a Ninja. It was so cool! I always wanted to try it. Watch this fellas!'

I reckon Kingy and I is both stone-cold sober the second we realise what's happenin'. He's about to karate chop it, and it might not be the bear trap he thinks it is but he's gonna at least lose a few fingers.We both lunge at him at the same time, tryin' to stop him from settin' off the pressure plate.

SNAP!

Me blood runs cold at the sound and both Kingy and I close our eyes. I don't wanna see it. After a coupla seconds,

Hot Rocks

I open one eye. Davo's staring at us and he looks confused and a bit angry.

'Youse bloody missed it!' he shouts. 'That's like the most Ninja thing I ever done and you two old dickheads are standin' there with yer eyes closed' Davo slings the rabbit trap over his shoulder and stamps up the stairs. 'Now no-one's gonna believe me when I tell 'em at the pub. Pair a bloody drongoes, that's what youse are.'

After he's gone, me and Kingy just look at each other

'How'd he do that, Boss?'

'I dunno mate. I dunno.'

We's thinkin' about it when Mick comes stumblin' down the stairs. 'Look what I got, Boss! There's a whole fucken load of em out the back.'

'What are they, Mick? Mushrooms? Are ya bloody mad, mate? We're already on rum rations and you wanna go trippin', too?'

'I'll give 'em to Davo, eh Boss? He'll cook up a killer feed.'

'Are you sure about 'em, Mick?' says Kingy, 'I don't want us gettin' sick, mate.'

'I been gettin' bush tucker round here for twenty years, ya dickhead. I know a toadie when I see one. These are kosher. Gonna be a good feed.' Davo doesn't seem happy about the mushies but he takes 'em anyway. We slow down a bit for the rest of the arvo; the booze is starting to take a toll but we're pretty much done, except for the vat.

'Okay Boss, double drinking time!' says Kingy, rubbing his hands. He's enjoying this rum way too much. The rest of us is feeling pretty green. We've had enough to last a bloody lifetime. Kingy estimates about 20 litres in the last coupla days. If we wasn't real men, we'd be dead by now. I go down with Kingy to check the vat. We can move it a bit now and the weird rattling noise is louder, too, sending a chill up me spine. I decide I ain't gonna drink anymore. I reckon I know what's inside but I ain't tellin' the boys.

'So what's in there, Boss?'

'I dunno mate. Probably just the stopper,' I says, and Kingy gives me a funny look. We fill up all the glasses and wobble upstairs where Davo's cookin' up dinner.

'Are ya sure about this, Mick?'

'For fuck's sake, just cook 'em up, Davo. I know what I'm doing!' Davo ain't happy but he cooks Mick up a mushie omelet after the rest of us have finished. I sneak off to bed while the others are hammering into the rum. It's been a good job, I thinks, and I'm smiling as sleep catches up with me. I really love those boys.

DAY THREE

I snap awake in the early hours to the sound of screaming. I look around. Davo looks scared real bad and Mick and Kingy ain't in their swags.

Hot Rocks

'Fucken' spiders. I hate fucken' spiders, get em off me!' Kingy is standing in the hallway swiping at his arms. I slap him hard on the face and he stops, peering at me.

'Jesus, Kingy. What're ya doin?'

'Oh, g'day, Boss. What's up?' He's slurring badly and he can barely stand and his eyes are focused about a metre to my left. I wave my hand in front of him and he doesn't register.

'Can you see me, Kingy?'

'Course not, it's pitch black in here, Boss.' The hall light is on and there's plenty of light.

'Okay, mate, I think it's bedtime now.' I take him by the hand and lead him back to his swag, kicking over his glass of rum meanwhile. Davo is staring wide-eyed. 'Kingy's been up all night, drinkin' that bloody rum. I think he's gone blind,' I whisper to him. Davo shakes his head. Kingy's asleep before I leave the room, drooling into the pillow.

I go looking for Big Mick and find him in the bathroom. He's curled up naked, spew and everythin' all over the walls and floor. He looks up at me with red eyes. 'I think them mushies was a bit wrong, Boss,' he croaks at me. Gagging from the smell, I help him into the bath and turn on the shower so he don't dehydrate.

I can't deal with this right now, I thinks to meself. *I've had enough, I reckon.*

'Get up Davo!' We're going right now! I'm fucken sick of this. Get those two bloody idiots in the back of the truck and put down a bucket and some plastic sheeting.' While he does this I aim the pressure hose at the bathroom and clean it all up as good as it's gonna get.

I coil up the hose and go outside. Davo takes off his gloves; he's leaning on the back of the truck. 'What about the bathroom, Boss?'

'Done and dusted mate. We're gone.' With that, I slam down the door of the truck and then there's an almighty scream. Davo goes white as a sheet. His finger's caught in the door. I try to open the truck door but, as I'm flicking the handle, Davo faints and falls backwards. I hear a weird popping noise and blood sprays out of his finger socket in an arc. Davo hits the deck and starts whimpering, blood spurting from his new stump in time with his heartbeat. I quickly grab his finger outta the door and take off my shirt and wrap it around his hand.

'I'm sorry Davo,' I say, as I help him into the cab. He's just staring at his hand in shock. I pop his finger into my pocket.

I've got one more thing to do before the job's finished. I grab the crowbar and heads downstairs. In the grey light of the coming dawn, I attack the vat of rum. I hit it over and over. The bastard thing has been mocking me for days and I beat the shit out of it. There's rum and sweat and blood all over me by the time I finish smashing it.

'Fuck you!' I say to it. Now that it's dead and the rum is gone into the earth and all over me, I look into the vat. I have to know what's in there. I just stare gobsmacked.

Hah! That's not what I expected, I say to myself. It's like a weight has lifted off me and I whistle as I saunter to the truck to take the boys to hospital.

It's been a good job.

'Well done, boys,' I say, as I start the truck and head off down the drive.

Blink

Denise Delaney

I used to create things ... now I think.
Me, the geek, or is it the gink?

I loved to dance, now I drink.
No more hip swing on offer, no surreptitious wink,
just a twirl of my glass. Ice cubes go chink.

I hugged trees, fought whalers and the wearing of mink,
maintaining the rage, then, into apathy I did slink.

I once was tall, now I shrink.
Limbs moving slowly, joints crunch and then clink.

For a while, me and he were a DINK.
Now it's a pension, and I'm on the brink
of washing my hands of it all. Life is a fink.

I tremble inside, shake my head, I blink
and I'm 13 again. Pretty in pink.

Half a House

Diane Jensen

Well, there it was: half a house just delivered. I now had a lounge room, kitchen and toilet, at last, after 15 years, four kids, numerous pets, and thousands of head of cattle. Now I just needed the bedrooms and bathroom. They were on the way. It was hard to contain my excitement in anticipation of a real house; a proper home to hold back the gritty dust and weather.

The truckie, having unloaded his cargo, headed over to the machinery shed for a feed and a beer or two. Grinning, my husband Rob also went over to join the workers in the shed. A shiny-beaded, sweating 18-gallon keg awaited the thirsty men. Sometimes I joined Rob in a beer, as I intended to now. During the previous years of our station life though, I was either pregnant or breast-feeding our latest addition.

Over those years, we grubbed around and made do in an 18-foot caravan with an 'always only temporary' multi-coloured tin lean-to adjoining it. This three-and-a-half-sided structure leant precariously up against the caravan. I hated it. Gazing over there, I could feel myself slipping into the memories of past hazards with this structure. The lean-to captured and held the heat of an overbearing sun. It froze anything inside in the winter. Lashed down though, it bravely stood as an adjunct to the caravan, withstanding fierce land gales, choking dust and thundering, crackling electrical storms. Somehow, it held fast against anything the climate threw at us, demanding occasional running repairs.

Sometimes, I would also feel a little fond of the lean-to, mainly because it was a survivor, like me. It had bruises and dents, holes and rusted sides that slammed around in the winds. Some of the tin came from old abandoned mine shafts. There were two doors salvaged from the outside dunnies of a pub, rotting 60 ks away in the scrub. Rob secured these relics to the tin sheets and decided to brighten them up with red paint. I smiled at his enthusiasm. I was weary and tired with swollen feet, carrying our second boy into the eighth month. At this stage I really didn't care much about coloured doors!

The day he began to paint we were hit with a sudden hailstorm, which belted onto the tin sheeting, creating a cacophonous racket, ending the paint job for that day and evermore. Other important issues claimed the attention of my husband.

This was all history now, as I gazed delightedly at my new half-a-house. Up to this point, other needs for our growing cattle station had been prioritised. The big shed, housing feed and machinery, was first to be built. Then followed fences, two dams, more cattle yards, more stock and medical and vet's bills. We knew it would be a struggle and it was, but we held fast to our dreams.

Excitement was building in me as we anticipated the arrival of the second truck bringing my bedrooms and bathrooms. I could hardly wait. The men laughed at me as I did little jigs of joy, swirling the dust at my feet. I could barely contain my eagerness for a whole proper home after all this time. It was almost too much to bear. Even the kids jumped around, shrilling with excitement and questions.

Over the years, amongst all the other demands of life on our growing cattle station, growing children, and School of the Air lessons, I nurtured and gradually increased to one acre, an organic herb and vegetable garden. This was my special project. Now I'd reached the stage of marketing to outlets through the small network of organic growers. It fed my soul and helped temporarily to separate me from the constant demands of our station life. I carted the fruits of my labour in our short-wheel based Landie, which was many years into old age and held together with bits of wire and all manner of makeshift parts. I was never sure if I would reach my destination and return without mishap! Though the Landie was banged up, dented, dirty, and scarred with gouges, the outline of Australia was still visible on the front doors. This outline was a reminder of our previous wandering, carefree days.

Rob's grandfather had died a year ago, not long after doing up his grand old Queenslander house. He left that beautiful house to us in his will. We always enjoyed long comfort rests there during our travels. Now here it was – well half of it anyway. I skipped past the new half-house and headed to the keg for a beer.

Suddenly the shed's short-wave radio crackled and burst into life. Rob put down his beer and crossed the shed to answer it. It was loud. It's always loud so we can hear it wherever we are on the station. 'High Peaks', our neighbouring cattle station one hundred kilometres away, was calling.

As we all I listened in, I felt as though I was moving in slow motion: my legs buckled beneath me and my beer slipped out of my hand. I did not want to hear anymore. 'High Peaks' was calling to inform us that the second truck carrying the other half of granddad's house had just plunged 900 metres down Grundy's Escarpment.

The Tip of the Iceberg

Stella Perkins

1992

Beverley took a slow sip of her Vienna coffee. She was sitting in a little coffee shop in the Queen Victoria Arcade in Sydney with her old school friend, Eunice Sutton. Beverley and Eunice were once the closest of friends but these days they only saw each other once a year when Beverley came down to the city for her specialist's check-up. Beverley had been listening to Eunice's story about the last days of her mother's life. It had been the most newsworthy event of the year for Eunice and it meant she was no longer tied down to nursing her aged mother. Eunice could now pick up the threads of her own life and pursue her heart's desires.

'What is it that you really want to do now, Eunice? I know you were once interested in writing. Is this the direction you plan to follow?'

'At last I can start to write the book I always knew I would one day write. I've booked myself in for a writers' retreat in the Blue Mountains where I'll spend ten glorious days writing under the tutor they've selected. I can't wait. But what about you Beverley, how are your parents and what have you been up to this last twelve months?'

Beverley thought, as she licked the chocolate from around the rim of her coffee cup. 'I never see my folks these days Eunice. I've wiped all ties with them. I still see my brother and sister occasionally but after that affair with the travelling carnival crowd, I can't be bothered with Mum and Dad. I'm so disappointed in them.'

Eunice looked at Beverley's face. The sadness she saw there was a revelation to her. Beverley had never spoken so frankly about her parents in all the time Eunice had known her and that was a total of almost 20 years. Time had left its mark on the once-lovely face. Beverley had taken up smoking after she left school and began University; her voice had that low, deep, throaty and somewhat sexy tone to it that many smokers' voices have and the wrinkles around her eyes and mouth indicated a rather cynical outlook on life. Eunice, who had been feeling as though her own life was at last just beginning, wondered if her friend was suffering from depression.

'I've been waffling on for the last half hour about my troubles and my life. Let's catch a ferry over to Manly and you can tell me all about yours. Now that I'm going to be a proper writer I need to draw from a collection of stories.'

The women paid their bill and left the tiny crowded café to catch a taxi to the Quay, from which the ferries to Manly were departing. Alighting from the taxi, Beverley breathed in the fresh, salty air.

'I never get tired of this trip on the ferry. I only go about once a year when we meet up but this is something I always love.'

Hot Rocks

'Let's find a seat at the front in the sunshine and you can begin your story. What happened with the carney people? I had no idea you were linked to that crowd. They're a pretty closed group aren't they?'

As soon as they were seated out on the deck, Beverley took a cigarette from her capacious bag, lit up and took a deep breath. 'You remember when I was in second year at high school, I ran away from home and was gone for the whole of third term?'

'It was always a mystery what happened to you. Rumours ran rife. Some people said you were pregnant and had to have an abortion, others said you were in a home for delinquents. Susan Thomas said you had TB and had to be isolated in hospital.'

Beverley shook her head and laughed. 'There is no lack of imagination there,' she said. 'No, I just joined the circus.'

Eunice looked fascinated. 'I've always dreamed of joining the circus. Were you a trapeze artiste?'

'Nothing so glamorous; I helped run the dodgem cars. It was terrible, but I was madly in love with the young fellow who helped with the dodgems and we shared a caravan with three other kids.'

'Those vans aren't exactly huge. It must have been really cramped.'

'Cramped and dirty and smelly, but when you are young and madly in love you see things differently.'

'Your parents must have been frantic. Did they know where you were?'

'I rang them after I'd been gone for about six weeks when the glow began to fade and the reality and squalor set in. By that time, I was already drug dependent and I realised I was being groomed for a prostitution racket.'

'You're making this up aren't you?' Eunice could hardly believe what Beverley was telling her. It seemed an unlikely story for the tame, quiet kid that Beverley had been at school. 'So Beverley, what did your parents do to make you feel so bitter towards them? Didn't they come rushing to your rescue?'

Beverley crushed out her cigarette and put the butt neatly away in a special gold box, in the same way she had hidden this secret part of her life from friends and associates. 'That's just it Eunice. They came in the dead of night, dragged me out of the caravan and, with hardly a word, dropped me off at this rehab centre where I spent the next six weeks alone, terrified and sick to my stomach, with drug addicts and alcoholics who were all older than I was. I can never forgive them for being so heartless.'

'What happened when you went back home? I remember you came back to school and you seemed to be exactly the same as you'd always been. Didn't everything go back the way it used to be?'

'There was always this barrier between us. I was like a prisoner in my own home. They never trusted me again and I for sure never really trusted them. Any normal parents would have hugged their child and told them they loved them but my parents could hardly bear the sight of me. I left home at the first opportunity.' Beverley lit up another cigarette and took a deep draw.

'But Bev. At least they saw that you went to rehab and came off the drugs; surely that was a sign they cared about you?'

Beverley blew smoke out through her nostrils. 'I think they just wanted to be sure I didn't contaminate my little brother and sister with my wild ways.' Dark clouds blocked out the sun and the wind began to blow. The two women quickly made their way down the steps and into the cabin. Beverley picked up a newspaper from the seat and began to read as though she wished she had never spoken of the great secret.

'Listen,' said Eunice, concerned with her friend's state of mind. 'Just stay there, I'll get us both a coffee.'

Beverley flicked through the newspaper. Her attention was captured by an article showing a photo of a couple who reminded her of her parents. The article read:

> Cold-case detectives are questioning a middle-aged couple about the murder of three people whose bodies were found in a burnt-out caravan twenty years ago. The couple, Alex and Maude Sutton, maintain it was not murder but a 'service to humanity, ridding the world of scum.' 'Those evil people,' Mrs Sutton told our reporter, 'kidnapped my

daughter, introduced her to heroin and
were threatening to lead her into a
life of prostitution. My daughter was
just the tip of the iceberg; there were
many other young people who were
enticed into this terrible racket. We
only did what any parent would do to
make sure children are protected.'

Beverley's mind was racing. She had cut all ties with her family and the police would be hard-pressed to trace her. She knew they would be looking for her because her side of the story would reveal answers that no-one, not even her parents, knew. Eunice was the only person from her past who could reveal the connection. Her brother and sister did not know where she lived and they had no idea she had completely changed her identity. The only link was Eunice, and Beverley cursed herself for breaking a lifetime habit of silence in regard to her story. She looked up to see Eunice coming towards her with the two coffees in a carry-box.

Beverley half rose to take the coffee from Eunice and at the same time she tucked the newspaper under her bum and sat on it. 'Thanks, Eunice. You're too nice, Eunice.' They both smiled as they shared that old school-time joke on Eunice's name. As she sipped the coffee, Beverley thought how synchronistic it was that they were together on a ferry in the middle of the harbour when she discovered the police would be searching for her. Surely it was a sign to act quickly.

Hot Rocks

'Let's go back on deck again, Eunice. I need a smoke before we leave the ferry.' The rain had stopped but the sudden squalls of wind sent the boat rocking. The ferry master was having problems lining the boat up with the dock. All eyes were on the fast-approaching wharf and the speed of the ferry. The two women stood by the rail. 'Just look at the lovely deep green colour of that water, Eunice. Are my eyes the same colour?'

Eunice looked up into Beverley's eyes and received a head-butt that knocked her out. Beverley scooped her up and tossed her overboard, just as the ferry master put the boat into reverse. The sudden movement threw a number of passengers off-balance and kept the attention away from Eunice's splash as she landed in the backwash of the propellers.

Beverley did not hang about but joined the crowds waiting to disembark. She planned to purchase different clothes from the second-hand shop nearby, change her hairstyle, her name, travel to a regional town, like Wagga Wagga, where she would find work and rent a place to live. She would leave her old life behind and continue to live with no regrets, one day at a time, especially now she had another death behind her.

The Invisible Woman

Stella Perkins

2017

A grey day on the harbour. No one noticed the thin, stooped woman in the pale grey coat. The gulls swooped and screamed as the wind caught their wings. The crowd boarding the ferry pushed and shoved its way up the gangplank. The woman in grey patiently waited by the high wire fence until most of the people were gone, then she made her way down the companionway to the cabin below, smoothing her grey hair as she sat alone on the bench. Young people in their bright clothes laughed and jostled each other and navigated their way towards the deck where they leaned over the rail, watched the water and the detritus of civilisation float away.

The woman in grey sat almost invisible in the lower cabin on board the Cremorne ferry. Once, Beverley had been a bright, happy young person just like those noisy teenagers. She watched and smiled wryly to herself. She had learnt her lesson and now she worked hard to maintain her cloak of invisibility. It suited her to dress in vague dull colours, to wear her hair neat, short and grey, to drift with the flow of the crowds, never drawing attention, never standing out from the city multitudes.

Hot Rocks

She travelled by public transport, she worked in boring clerical jobs, changed her place of work every two years and did not become friends with anyone. She had lots of acquaintances but she could never risk another close friendship. Not anymore. She never lived in pleasant communities but sought anonymous apartment living where she was unnoticed. It was hard work staying invisible, never eye-balling anyone, never accepting invitations, never doing actions by rote. It was important not to be predictable, so she did not sit in the same train carriage regularly, she always travelled to work by different routes and she never ate lunch in the same place. It took careful planning and studying to make it work. She could not ever let her guard down.

Sometimes, she longed to take a painting class or to learn yoga but these were the dubious luxuries of normal people. Dull routine could only be enjoyed in isolation. In her boring unit she watched horror movies and serials, or read books purchased from second-hand stores. But whenever Beverley was out in public, she was careful to visit different stores and enjoy coffee in as many different cafes as she could find. It was the price of a youth spent wildly; it was the consequence of actions from years past.

Christmas and Easter were particularly hard but she had been fortunate to discover the celebrations the God-botherers gave to the homeless. Here the city's anonymous, amorphous, strange and queer folk were treated to concerts and dinners by the Great and Good carrying out their paternalistic duties. Beverley had learnt the shuffle, the downcast eyes, and the humble mumble of thanks when alms were graciously delivered. On odd occasions she changed tack and became one of the benevolent beings just to add confusion and unpredictability to the mix.

It was a difficult task and she could not afford to get sick so Beverley took very good care of herself. It was a life of non-attachment, of no possessions and no people. But Beverley did have a family once. She knew what it was to love and to hate and to stand up for what you believed in. She knew what it was like to be betrayed, too. To be rejected and to be cast aside and thrown out with the rubbish. It was difficult not to help people who begged for assistance. Beverley knew she could never allow herself to soften and hold out a hand to someone weaker than herself. She had to be as hard as nails if she were to survive.

To overcome her natural need to reach out, to touch another person, she had found that random acts of kindness helped. Beverley wrote an anonymous blog where she gave advice to the desperate. In the city, she used computers in many public places, public libraries, community centres and stores, but never from her place of work. She was very careful to use facilities that could not be traced back to her. Her following was the huge tribe of underground wanderers populating the big cities, the park dwellers, the homeless, the mentally ill and the addicts, the shadows, the people who did not want to be found. Beverley shared tips for survival with them and they, in turn, exchanged theirs. They knew the skips where good, edible food could be sourced, where a free shower was available. She told where shelter from the cold could be found and where to find a listener to share a problem or two.

There was a problem occurring right now, on the deck where the young people had interrupted an old couple and hasty words were being exchanged. Beverley said to herself, 'Not my circus, not my monkeys.' And talking about monkeys, that little boy belonging to the mother who was giving all her attention to her phone, was enjoying himself swinging and climbing all over everything and everyone. What a little monkey he was.

The ferry was approaching the wharf, the people gathered their gear, the crew stood ready to secure the ferry with the guy ropes. This was the part Beverley hated. She was tense, held her breath while the pounding motor braked, remembering what she had done all those years ago. She saw the little monkey watching the young people preparing to jump from the ferry to the dock before the gangplank was in place. *Watch him mother* she thought to herself, but mother's eyes were still glued to her phone. One young fellow made the jump, then another and the little monkey slipped off the rail and fell into the turbid green waters. Drowning is a silent death as Beverley well knew. *Not my monkey* said her head but her heart screamed *Save him*!

Almost without thinking, Beverley jumped in after him. The water was so murky she could hardly see him. She dived down again searching, grasping for the opportunity she had let pass all those years ago. *I wish I had not turned away.* She caught a glimpse of his white shirt and reached for it, slipped her arm around his tiny body and pushed his head above the water. He began to cough and Beverley breathed a sigh of relief.

The crowd cheered when Beverley came up from the cloudy green with the little monkey and delivered him to his mother. They fussed and declared her to be the hero of the day. She tried desperately to escape their attention and, while all eyes were on the dramatic reunion of the mother and son, Beverley slipped away.

She stood motionless beneath the wharf, still and grey as one of the grey pylons holding the wharf in place. Above her she heard the clamour of the crowd as they searched for her, then a voice: 'She's vanished into thin air,' followed by another: 'Not to worry, I've got a photo of her on my phone.'

Damn. All those years of sacrifice wasted and all because she had followed her heart. Now what? If the press and the police find her...leaning against the pole, Beverley watched the tide dissipate and wished she could dissipate with it. Well there was nothing else for it. It was time to vanish again. She waited under the wharf for an hour until she had dried out enough to look normal. She had to change her appearance immediately. She had left the coat behind on the ferry when she jumped. Was there anything in her pockets to betray her? Only money and her ferry ticket. Because of her years of practice, her money was safe in a water-tight belt close to her skin. She had enough to buy a secondhand jumper and a newspaper and a bus fare. She could never return to her basement flat at Cremorne. It would have to be abandoned. Tonight she could use one of the St Vincent de Paul missions for the homeless until she could gather her resources together. She could kill for a hot black coffee. She smiled at that thought. She had killed for less before. Never mind, a luke-warm instant from the mish would have to do instead.

Beverley made her way to the bus stop. She had dried out by now but her hair needed combing and her shoes were still squishy. Lucky that she hadn't lost a shoe in the water, that would have made her stand out from the crowd. The motion of the bus, the warmth and the feeling of enclosure made her sleepy and she began to drift off. She shook her head. She had to stay alert, at least until she was safely at the mission.

At last, she sat among the many faceless people, sipping her coffee. Across from her was a drunk recovering from a bender and an old couple huddled together. They reminded her of that photo in the newspaper she'd hidden from Eunice on their last ferry ride together, the photo of her parents being charged with burning a caravan with the bodies of the three people Beverley had killed, over twenty years ago. Her parents were still in gaol, or were they? How long ago was that? Surely not another twenty years had passed while she flitted from place to place, evading discovery.

The cup in her hand began to shake. She couldn't stop shivering. The old couple were watching her now but she couldn't control her shaking.

'Are you all right?' asked the old lady. Beverley shook her head. 'I'll get some help.' And the old lady vanished. Vanishing was Beverley's trick. She had to regain control. She stood to move away but her legs gave beneath her. The old man came and helped her back to the chair. He said nothing but placed a hand on her shoulder. She knew he knew who she was. She could feel the recriminations through his hand. The old lady returned with the medical officer who realised Beverley was suffering from shock and put her to bed, dressing the nasty cut she'd received from the oyster shells when she rescued her monkey.

The old man took the old lady by the hand. 'Come along Maude, it is not our circus, not our monkey.' And he tried to draw her away from Beverley.

Hot Rocks

Then she knew without a doubt: it was them. They had lived by that saying. She couldn't help herself. She cried out, 'Mum!'

'She's delirious,' murmured the old man pulling the old lady from the room.

'No! It is our Beverley, God has delivered her to us here in his Mission House. God be praised.' The old lady knelt beside Beverley, crying, but the old man stood back near the door watching, shaking his head.

'Come away Maude, no good can come of this. Come away.'

It was too late. There was no dragging the old lady away now. For years Maude had dreamt of meeting up with Beverley again, of holding her close once more. The old man, separated all those years from his devoted wife, cursed Beverley every day of his incarceration, while they paid for something of which they were innocent and their daughter ran free. He could never forgive her for depriving him of his beloved Maude and now that he had her back, Beverley was claiming all her attention and affection.

Beverley looked up from her mother's embrace to see the look on her father's face and she knew she could never regain the family feeling she had rejected when she ran away from home to join the circus. The trust was gone. It was time to move on. Gently she moved out from her mother's arms.

'Thank you for helping me. I will be fine now, but my name is not Beverley and I do not know you. You have mistaken me for someone else. My name is Eunice and I must be getting along. I hope you find your daughter one day.'

The next day she caught the Overlander to another state and vanished. She never saw her parents again. It was the least she could do for them.

The Ocean

Denise Delaney

A god sleeps in the deep blue.
The ocean.
Placid. Calm. Glassy. Still.
A mirror for a feeding bird
skimming and soaring,
drawing lines of undulating hills
that linger in the air.

The god stirs.
A lightning flash and a thunderclap
cleaves the azure sky.
Roiling clouds darken the heaven's vast expanse,
a charcoal grey tidal wave
slinging light-filled sheets
and golden tines violently down.
Seething. Advancing. Invading.
The churning sea drums
a tumultuous rhythm,
then dances.
Indigo depths rising, colliding,
flinging iridescent spume
high into the air,
Pounding a flamenco in navy and white.
Shaping. Thundering.
Dissolving.
The god settles to sleep.

An azure sky appears.
A bird skims a gentle sea.
Placid. Calm. Glassy. Still.

The Baseball Game

Lucy Powter

It was the day of the semi-finals for our town's baseball team. They had to win to qualify for the grand final the following week and Adam Johnson was ready. He had trained and played since leaving school about seven years previously and wanted to prove he was a good pitcher and captain. He was also aware that should his secret weakness be exposed, it might destroy the camaraderie – as it had done with a previous team. Adam was looking forward to meeting up with Jerry Farmer at the dressing shed. He had joined up last year as the catcher for the team. Once he'd been a rival, but now they were great mates. Jerry was the only person who knew Adam's weakness. He was fully supportive in helping Adam overcome his problem and had vowed never to reveal it.

There was a loud cheer from the huge crowd as the two teams ran onto the oval. A hush descended as the two captains faced one another. The umpire tossed the coin, Adam won and the crowd cheered again. He chose to bat first. He knew his team could bat well if nerves did not get to them and so he would be able to judge how good the other side was at fielding. Also, he would be able to assess the pitcher.

Hot Rocks

The game started. Mary, Adam's wife, seated behind the wire fence which was between her and Jerry, anxiously watched as Adam took his position on the batting team. She thought how handsome he was with his short dark hair beneath his baseball cap, his brown eyes and caramel skin. His close-fitting uniform clung to him, showing off his tall, lean physique.

The game continued. Each innings was exciting, the scores fluctuating and the crowd roaring as one after another batsman was caught out or a home run was batted.

Now it was the seventh innings. This could be the last one, Mary thought, as she looked at Jerry crouched behind the batter's plate. He had his facemask over his head, chest plate on and his catcher's mitt covered his right hand. He was ready. Behind him stood the umpire fully outfitted in black, mask and all. Mary watched as Adam took his position on the pitcher's mound. Jerry viewed Adam through the bars of his mask as he made ready for his wind up, ball in hand. Adam touched his right arm with two fingers before he let the pitch go. Jerry read the signal ... watch the batter on second base! The batsman held the bat in front just as the ball hit, it was a bunt, landing a few feet in front of him; he then ran to first base just as Jerry picked it up, straightened, and threw it to second base where the runner was trying to steal. He was out! The crowd roared. One down two more to go.

Hot Rocks

Jerry crouched down slamming his fist into the catcher's mitt, his muscles tensed. He was ready. They needed two more out and they had the semi. There was a runner on first and now a new batter faced Adam. He watched as if in slow motion, as Adam released the ball. Jerry knew from experience where the ball was going to go and he was waiting. The ball slammed into the bat, a high one, but Jerry caught it, stepped sideways and threw it to second base catching out the runner. Both out! The crowd roared and clapped. They had won! They were in the grand final. Jerry, Adam and the team jumped around excitedly slapping one another on the back, grinning and shouting. As they walked towards the dressing shed, Jerry thought he and Adam were a good pair. The passion they had for baseball was stronger each time they played.

In the dressing sheds, the players cheered, talked loudly, jostled one another in various stages of undress, discussing many aspects of the game. 'Hogwash!' was heard above the din. All looked to see where this had come from. It was the manager.

'It was the pitch Adam threw in the seventh innings that won us the game.'

'No, it was because he was sober for a change!' yelled a voice. Adam froze. The coach ignored the remark and said he agreed Adam's pitch was great but it was Jerry who won the game catching that ball on the full and then throwing it to second base.

'We now have a great chance at winning the grand final.'

Adam let out a deep breath. He and Jerry winked and smiled at one another as they sat down and shared a well-earned lemonade.

Postcard from Liverpool

Robin Hammond

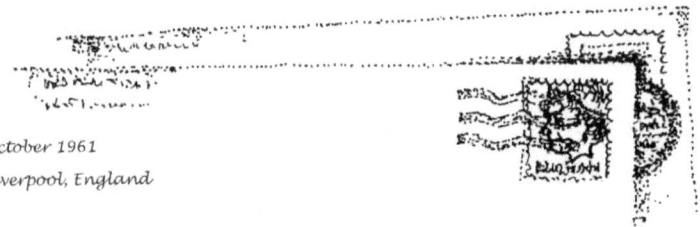

October 1961
Liverpool, England

Hi Mum and Dad:

Here I am in England!! Trip over on the ship was great; met lots of fab people. We're living in digs in Liverpool and having a fab time. Last night we heard a band called The Beatles playing something called Merseybeat music; don't think they'll make it to the big time but they were quite good. Going to somewhere called Carnaby Street tomorrow. Should be fab.

Love to all Downunder,
Sally

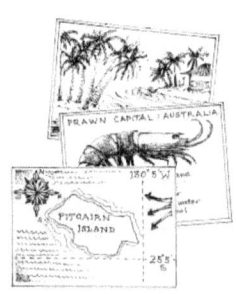

The Lucky Spin

Terry Dunkley

It was Friday evening at the club, the only evening I went out by myself.

'You gonna have another round?' asked my mate Johnno.

'Nah! I've only got five bucks left.'

The situation was that my wife handled all the finances as she was much better at it than I was, and with two daughters and a sizeable mortgage to repay, she worked things out very well. My pay was transferred into our joint account, which I didn't have access to, and every Friday evening she would give me twenty dollars to have a drink with my friends.

'Listen mate,' said Johnno, 'if you're that skint, stick it in the pokies and see what comes up.'

'I've never played them in my life, in fact I wouldn't even know where to put the money in, and the missus is always telling me what a curse they are.'

'Don't worry about the missus; come on I'll show you, it's dead easy and you might get lucky.' Johnno steered me to the gambling section and to a vacant machine. 'Stick your note in there.' The machine snatched the note from my hand before I could change my mind.

'What's next Johnno?'

'You've only got five bucks so let's make it a dollar a bet. Now press this button and see what comes up.' I watched the credit go down, four, three, two, one, and then the machine played a jingly tune for us and announced that I had twenty free spins.

'Good on yer, mate, you're on a roll.' Before long the machine went crazy with sound and flashing lights. 'Congratulations, mate, you've just won the jackpot of seven hundred and fifty dollars, go over to the teller and he'll pay you in cash.'

It felt really strange having all that money in cash and in my pocket and very elevating.

'You need to keep going when you're on a winning streak,' said Johnno, 'but pick another machine as this one won't pay another jackpot for a time.'

It wasn't long before I won another jackpot, and now my adrenaline was running really high and I was shaking all over.

'With your luck,' said Johnno, 'you should be with the high rollers. Come on let's go to the casino.'

It was three a.m. when I arrived home.

'Where have you been?' demanded my anxious wife. I told her all about the evening and how I had won enough money to pay off the mortgage. Her face softened.

'That's wonderful!' she exclaimed. 'Where is it?'

'Where's what?'

'The money.'

'Lost!'

'What do you mean, lost? Where did you lose it?'

'In the machine, it all went back into the machine.' That was when my wife became demented and used language that I'd never heard her use before. 'It's okay, love,' I tried to assure her. 'If I've done it once I can do it again. Give me twenty dollars and I'll do it again tonight.'

You know, I never saw that saucepan coming.

Food for Thought

Diane Jensen

The unease I often felt in his presence prickled at me again, as I followed him from the lift to his tenth floor apartment. He'd met me on the ground floor to escort me up.

'I've got your favourite wine,' he stated, looking directly into my eyes.

Was that a glint of desire I saw? I wondered. God no, please not! I opened my mouth to thank him and then clamped it shut. How did he know what my favourite wine was? Has he been following me? On several previous occasions, I had refused his dinner invitations, claiming our work-related status as a reason for my refusals. Thinking I had put him off, it took me by surprise when now, some months later, he repeated the invitation.

My curiosity piqued, I accepted, though I had a sense of foreboding immediately. Damn, I thought. Too late now to pull out. It was his son's 13th birthday, he explained. A special occasion on the eve of complicated teen years. I tried to shake off the feeling of apprehension. After all, there would be a young boy present. Having two teenagers myself and a husband long gone, as a single parent I felt empathy for him. He had some time ago told me, while we were both in the office coffee room, his wife had disappeared several years before, and made no further contact with him. As I hadn't invited any personal confidences from him, I felt embarrassed and gave a non-committal reply. However, until this recent invitation, I was unaware there was a son from the marriage.

He was a closed sort of man at work, intelligent in his job, charming at times and pleasant-looking, though his fathomless eyes often looked haunted and obsessive. Sometimes, in the office I would feel those eyes on me, but if I turned he would quickly look away or dazzle me with a smile.

'Shoes off please,' he said, as he guided me towards the room in which we were to dine. My uneasy feelings heightened. This first room was sparsely furnished, and didn't look at all lived-in. As we passed into the next room, I froze. It was almost barren! A long room, more the kind used as a rumpus room. My feet sank into plush, white carpet as I padded through. All walls and ceiling were white and I detected the odour of fresh paint.

'Have you just repainted here?' I asked, my stomach turning over. He seemed not to hear my question. Even as a child, I had hated the smell of fresh paint. My father used to say: 'Get over it.' I never did.

The walls had no adornment other than one long shelf on which was massed framed photographs of a young child from babyhood to about five years old, but nothing more recent. All were of his son, I assumed. Strange, there were no photos continuing into the child's recent years, and none of anyone else.

Adjacent to this shelf, was a set of floor-length, double French windows that were closed, and with a shudder I saw that outside they were covered in closely interlocked steel bars. We were on the tenth floor. Why were there bars? It wasn't possible for anyone to break in. No curtains framed the windows and I could see they led to a balcony.

I heard the click of a lock. He'd gone back to the door we had just come through. I hesitated and then glanced to a table that grabbed my attention. It was a small, rectangular shape, covered in a faded tablecloth with a design of teddy bears and racing cars. Surely a 13-year-old would have outgrown this. A large bowl of blood-red tomato sauce dominated one end of the table and was the only condiment. There were three place settings. The cutlery and plates sat on placemats shaped like green frogs. Fronting each placemat was a glass of bright green cordial. In the centre of the table was a birthday cake in the shape of a frog with white icing, adorned with green candles. I presumed, in my agitated state, there were 13 candles. The cake took obvious pride of place.

'Your son must be very fond of frogs,' I said. Again, he didn't answer, all the time smiling and moving about the room, appearing to check on things.

At the other end of the table, sat a gleaming, stainless steel warming oven. My eyes riveted on it and then I glanced back to the bowl of tomato sauce. I was speechless, even though a hundred questions swam through my brain. My host benignly sat me down on one side of the child-sized table. With a sweaty hand, I grabbed at the glass of awful cordial, swallowing quickly, to wet my constricted throat.

'Where is your son?' I asked.

'Oh, he'll be along shortly, when he is ready'. I felt a vague relief. He indicated the warming oven, telling me to help myself. As he opened it up, a nauseous odour and wafts of steam floated out, revealing a pile of long buns and six fat, red hot dogs.

'The wine?' I sputtered.

'Oh, we'll have that later when Jeremy goes to bed. Come on, eat,' he directed me. 'We always have my son's favourite food for his birthday.'

'But your son is not here yet,' I squeaked at him. He looked at me in surprise, as he placed a hot dog on the third plate and smiled at the chair in front of it.

'Of course he is, he just sat down. I knew the smell of hot dogs would bring him along'.

My jaw fell open as I stared at the empty chair and then down to one of the racing cars in the tablecloth, wishing the car was real and that I might be in it and out of here.

'You would be a good mother, I know it,' he said.

Hot Rocks

'Jeremy, this is Alice from the office. She is going to be your mother now. Alice this is my son Jeremy. Isn't he grown up? Aren't you going to wish him a happy birthday?'

Sour-tasting bile rushed up from my knotted stomach as I took in the empty chair, the disgusting, red hot dog placed carefully in the centre of the white plate, in front of the empty chair, and the barren room with a locked door and bars on the French windows.

'Jeremy had a little accident once,' he continued. 'This was his playroom, but he fell out of the windows and off the balcony. Now they are barred so it doesn't happen again. But you'll be here to look after him from today won't you?' he said, with confidence. 'No need to work at the office anymore.'

My brain was locked into one stupid thought. Did he want a live mother for his dead son, or a dead mother for his dead son?

A Boy Called Wayne

Robin Hammond

I was the first-born son of the family, so my Dad claimed naming rights.

He called me Wayne.

I was born in the late 70s and Wayne was not a name on everyone's list back then. My school was full of Damiens, Bradleys, Dylans, Andrews and Camerons. I was the only Wayne.

My father is a Western nut and he named me after his favourite cowboy actor: John Wayne. My younger brother's name is Clint and my mother called my sister Annie, after Annie Oakley; by then, even Mum was getting into the western theme. At least 'Clint' and 'Annie' have a bit of cool about them; there's no way you can make Wayne sound edgy.

Our house was full of cowboy crap. There was the horseshoe on the front door; the bleached buffalo horns on the front gate; the letterbox in the shape of a covered wagon. Shortly after we moved in, Dad dug up the whole front yard, covered it with sand and gravel and planted huge cactus plants in place of all the trees. He was trying to replicate the Arizona desert. He installed a cement Mexican sleeping under a big sombrero outside the front door and replaced Mum's garden gnomes with garishly-painted miniature donkeys pulling little carts, and cowboys swinging lariats. He even had a Red Indian creeping through the cactus, knife raised in one hand and a tomahawk in the other. There was nothing politically correct about my family. Living as we did in Coolangatta, it all looked just a little bit weird.

Dad only read Westerns and the bookshelves were packed with paperback cowboy stories: *Don't Die in Diablo; Noon Train to Wichita; Birth of a Gunfighter*. We ate hominy grits for breakfast and every weekend we slept in tepees, right up until I left home. For their 25th wedding anniversary, Dad and Mum, with much giggling, gave each other matching silver spurs. I lay awake that night, well into the early hours of the morning, listening to the jingling sounds coming from their room, interspersed with muffled cries of 'yee haw!' I was 17 at the time and my imagination ran riot; I hated to think what was going on in there.

So you can see why I was busting to leave home as soon as I'd finished school. I loved my Dad but I had a feeling there was a whole different world out there waiting for me.

Still, the apple doesn't fall far from the tree. What was I thinking when I asked my Dad his opinion on what I should do in the few months of freedom I had before starting uni the following year? He planted his feet firmly on the living room carpet, put one hand on his hip and gestured dramatically with a pointing finger: 'Go West Young Man!' he declared, in thrilling tones.

Sounded like a plan to me, so, while most of my mates were heading to Surfers for schoolies, I packed the old family station wagon, hung a horseshoe on the tow bar for luck and set out for Western Australia. My mate, Crazy Dave, rode shotgun – literally. He cradled an old hunting rifle and took potshots at crows as we rattled along. This was the mid-sixties and we were heading for the new mining boom in WA.

A few miles out of Broken Hill, our troubles began. The radiator boiled, the head gasket blew. The car was cactus. We began walking, hoping to hitch, but soon wandered off the track when Crazy insisted on stalking what he thought looked like a rabbit in the distance but turned out to be a dead log.

Then he vanished, to reappear twenty minutes later, minus his weapon but leading two mules. Turned out he'd come across an old prospector who fancied his rifle and offered to swap. 'We can ride them to WA,' he said, looking pleased with himself. 'They won't cost us nothing for fuel.'

'You dickhead!' I said. 'How's that gunna happen? Where's the riding gear, the saddles? All they've got is rope round their necks.'

Crazy got all defensive. 'Well, we can't leave them here. Maybe someone back in Broken Hill will buy them off us.'

'Fat chance!' I muttered, grabbing hold of one of the ropes.

So there we were, trudging through the outback, leading two reluctant mules, with no real idea of where we were going. We were thirsty, hungry and exhausted. And I hated those mules with a passion.

Towards midday, smoke appeared in the distance. 'That's all we need,' I said bitterly. 'A frigging bushfire.'

But Crazy, eager to redeem himself, grabbed my binoculars and hurried ahead. I followed with reluctance. 'It's not a bushfire, someone's got a barbecue going. It's a town!' called Crazy.

It was High Noon when we led the mules up the dusty main street of Silverton. The townsfolk gathered round in what I thought, with great naivety, was a welcoming attitude. Mighty friendly, I thought and held out my hand to the nearest moleskin-clad, sun-bronzed man-of-the-land: 'Howdy,' I said. He scowled in reply.

Turned out the mules had been stolen from one of the locals and they thought we'd done the stealing.

We spent the night in the lock-up while things were sorted out. My Dad drove down from the Gold Coast to collect us. I think he appreciated the chance to wear his favourite ten-gallon hat, blue jeans and checked shirt with monogrammed horseshoes.

After the paperwork was done, we stood on the front steps of the police station and, hangdog, I waited for Dad to bawl me out. He hooked his thumbs in his belt, squinted at the sun, then turned, tipping his hat in my direction. A slow smile spread across his face.

'Mule rustling, son,' he drawled. 'I'm proud of you.'

The Parkers

Terry Dunkley

Emily Parker hummed softly to herself as she placed the casserole in the oven. She thought of how her husband would appreciate it that evening. Emily was a quiet, unassuming person, forever putting herself last. She never argued with her husband, preferring to take evasive action rather than face him full-on. She tended to fade into the background, while he hogged the limelight.

The only time she had challenged him, was when he came home late after supposedly playing cribbage with his mate, with a faint smudge of lipstick on his shirt.

Vince Parker was the opposite of his wife. He was a bold-faced, lying, cheating, invective-spewing, short-tempered bully, with the soul of a black mamba. He believed that attack was the best form of defence. He had berated and castigated Emily for daring to even think he'd been with another woman.

Vince worked at the nuclear power station and because of his volatility, came to be known to his colleagues as 'The Reactor' – needing to be kept stable at all times. On several occasions, he had almost lost his job because of his bellicose manner, and if it hadn't been for the difficulty of replacing him, he would have been sacked long ago.

Hot Rocks

It was during one of these situations when senior management had upbraided him, that he left the plant in a thunderous mood, and driving the forty minutes home in peak traffic, he took to cursing aloud with bitter venom. Then another road user had the temerity to indicate and change lanes in front of him. Vince speeded up and hooted loudly on his horn, but he wasn't quick enough. The lane-changer had completed his legal manoeuvre and proceeded to give Vince the one-fingered saluted. Well, that was it. Vince drove forward to bump into his rear, causing the driver to pull over to the left. Vince pulled up behind him and in blind rage, got out of his own vehicle and strode forward to his adversary. This guy was going to know what real pain was. But when Vince opened the car door to drag him out, he was jabbed very squarely in the face by an iron steering wheel lock. With a cry of pain, Vince reeled backwards into the passing traffic and was hit by a large four-wheel drive. By the time the paramedics got him to hospital, he was well and truly dead.

Emily was wondering why her husband was late and what excuse he would make, when the sound of the doorbell made her jump. Wiping her hands on her apron, she opened the door to find two police officers standing on the steps.

'May we come in?' asked the male constable, removing his hat. 'I'm afraid we have some bad news for you.'

'Please do,' said Emily. 'What's happened?' She held open the door and they both entered.

'Would you like to sit down?' suggested the female officer. She then explained the circumstances as gently as she could and that they were holding a man at the station who was helping with their enquiries. 'We would like you to identify the body at some time,' the officer said.

'May I do it later?' replied Emily. 'I have so much on my mind, and I need to make some phone calls.'

'Of course. Perhaps we can pick you up at 10 a.m. tomorrow?'

'Yes, that will be fine.'

Emily closed the door quietly behind them, then smiled and hurried to her deceased husband's desk. Throwing papers everywhere, she found it. Yes! The will had not been changed and the life insurance premiums were up-to-date. She knew the terms of the insurance. A hundred thousand dollars immediately upon death, and the total amount within four weeks.

She made her first phone call.

'A1 Travel Centre?' She was about to do something her husband had forbidden. 'I'm glad I caught you. Could you book me a seat on the West Australian wildflower tour that's coming up in four weeks' time?' She settled back into the couch with anticipation. 'I have been thinking about doing this trip for years and now a window of opportunity has opened. I have a business matter to attend to tomorrow, but I'll be in to see you the following day.'

Emily Parker smiled to herself, as she took the casserole from the oven. *The Greek Islands*, she thought. *Maybe that will be my next adventure.* A long line of fun-filled years stretched ahead of her. She began singing: 'She's got the whole world, in her hands...'.

Poppy

Stella Perkins

'We are all going to your Pop's for lunch on Sunday.' Mum announced, one Wednesday at tea time.

'Aaw Mum! I've got netball training on then, so count me out.' I didn't want to go to Poppy's place on Sunday. Ever since Nan had died last year Poppy was fading away. I called him Poppy because he was like those poppies that droop their heads when they get old, lose their petals and all that polleny stuff goes everywhere. Poppy was like that these days. Tall and thin, he walked with his head down, watching the footpath, and his dark cardigan had a dusting of white dandruff all over the shoulders. You know how the stems of poppy flowers are all whiskery? That's how Poppy's cheeks felt whenever I had to kiss him. They scratched.

'I'm worried he's not eating properly and he is getting so lonely now that Nan's gone. Come on sweetheart, let's all show him how much we love him.'

'Mum, the last time I went there, he asked me to help him clean out the pantry.' He kept the medicine box at the top of the tallest shelf out of the reach of children. Now he had shrunk a bit, it was out of the reach of Poppy. 'You know that half of that medicine and most of the stuff in his pantry was older than I am? If we eat at Poppy's we risk getting poisoned.'

'I'm sure it can't be as bad as all that. We'll eat lots of the fresh vegetables he grows in his garden; now that will be healthy for everyone.'

'He keeps making these foghorn farts every time he bends down. He thinks no one can hear them but they're as loud as trumpeting elephants and they smell.'

As we drove to Poppy's place on a lovely sunny Sunday morning, Mum explained about deaf people. 'I know you get cross sometimes when Pop doesn't hear you when you talk to him, and he talks over the top of you when you're speaking, it's just that he's deaf and doesn't hear you unless you speak directly at him. If you turn away and he can't see your lips moving, he doesn't realise you are speaking.'

'I know that Mum but it just makes me cross.'

Dad piped up from the driver's seat: 'Another thing to remember is that he can't hear much if he's eating and listening at the same time.'

'Can't he multitask because he's a man?'

'Don't try to be funny,' Dad said, smiling. 'You try listening to the sounds in your head when you're eating. Give her one of those boiled lollies, Mother.' He paused to pass the packet of bullseyes to Mum. He always kept peppermint lollies in the car to eat on long car trips. While I munched and crunched on the hard lolly he said, 'See what I mean? It's hard to hear much over the loud sounds in your own head.'

'What's that dad? Can't hear a word you say.'

'Cheeky brat! Now one more thing to be expecting: deaf people often take over the conversation. Because they find it really hard to follow a conversation, they'll frequently introduce a favourite topic and talk on that for a while.'

'Ooh, yes! That makes me so mad.'

'Don't get cross about it. It's just a device to stay in the conversation. It's not that he's ignoring you. It's just that he can't hear you.'

'So if I turn my head away from the table and mutter, *I can't eat this food,* Poppy won't hear me?'

'I wouldn't bet on it,' replied Mum. 'Sometimes that hearing just seems to click back in and he hears the very thing you hoped he wouldn't.'

When we arrived at Poppy's house he was at the back door, waiting to greet us. He brushed his prickly cheek up against mine.

'Ouch!' I yelled, rubbing my cheek.

He grinned. 'I thought you'd like that. I kept them prickly just for you.'

'You wait. I'm going to raid your garden and eat all your fresh baby peas, just you wait and see. You won't have any left by the time I finish.' I planned to get full on baby peas to save being poisoned by Poppy's cooking. I loved

Hot Rocks

Poppy's garden: the peas, carrots and the smell of the tomato bushes when you brushed past them. Mum wandered through the garden with us but when Poppy bent to pull out a baby carrot he let out his foghorn blast and everyone ducked for cover.

'Lucky we're outside in the fresh air,' I murmured to Mum.

All too soon, we were seated around the dinner table. 'What's on the menu today Poppy?' I shouted.

'It is meatballs with surprises,' Pop replied, bringing out a steaming bowl of meatballs and another big bowl of spaghetti.

'What sort of surprises, Poppy?' I was a bit worried about Poppy's idea of a surprise. 'Will they be prickly like your whiskers?'

'It won't be a surprise if I tell you, now will it?'

'Yuk! What's this black thing?' I opened a meatball that was smothered in rich tomato sauce with a hint of balsamic and basil.

'You have struck the jackpot young'un. That is a black Kalamata olive. There are only a few of them. The others have cheese hidden inside them, some have a cherry tomato, some have peas that I collected before the Cannibal Kid arrived and ate all the babies in the garden.'

'Yum!' I yelled. 'This is better than finding money in the Christmas pudding. At least we can eat these surprises.'

Poppy smiled and Mum and Dad looked pleased. I tucked in and cleaned out my bowl. When I was sure Poppy could hear me, I looked straight at him and said. 'Thanks Poppy, I was afraid you might be a Crook Cook. But you are okay.'

Poppy smiled and said, 'Talking about Crook Cooks reminds me of the crookest cook I ever met. His name was Vincent Cook and he lived in Crookwell down near Goulburn in southern New South Wales.' Poppy stopped talking and looked at me.

'All right Poppy, we've all finished eating Tell me your Crookest Cook story.' Poppy was a great story teller. He made up the most frightful fibs. His stories were legend, like his farts.

'It was when I was driving trucks down in Victoria. We had this long, lonely stretch and Vincent Cook's Garage and Café were the last ones for miles. We had no choice but to call in there or starve. Vincent specialised in steak sandwiches but the steak was so tough, his customers used to yell, 'Why don't you mince it Vincent?' That's how he got named Mince-it-Vincent. See, what he used to do was listen in to the truckies talking and every time they mentioned they'd hit a kangaroo, he'd give his off-sider the nod and he'd head out and collect the road kill. Vincent figured after all that bashing of meat with a mallet to tenderise it, the steak must surely be worth a bang or two with a ten-ton truck. He also served up a mean toad-in-the-hole and his sweet of the day was a lovely spotted dick with custard.

'There's no such thing as toad-in-the-hole, is there Mum?'

'Yes indeed. It is baked sausages with a batter over the top. Spaces form in the batter and through the holes you can see the sausages poking through from the bottom of the dish.'

'But spotted dick, now that has to be made up. I mean that is disgusting!'

'Tell you what,' said Dad. 'How about next Sunday, we invite Pop to our place for lunch and your Mum will cook up a meal with toad-in-the hole and spotted dick pudding and custard, and you can invite that friend of yours from across the road to lunch?'

I smiled and nodded, but deep down I was thinking nobody would come to eat a meal like that. How wrong was I? On a freezing cold Sunday, we really enjoyed our steaming hot toad-in-the-hole with brussels sprouts and mashed sweet potato, followed by a steamed pudding spotted with currants and smothered with custard.

Water

Denise Delaney

I love swimming.

I love how with a flick of my tail I move forward, and with a double-flick go really fast.

Lucky I love swimming, 'cause water is essential. I must live in it or I will end up at that big, not-watery grave in the sky. It is fun living in my big bubble. I can see the world over and over again, watching it from sunrise to sunset.

I can see the small furry thing with pointed, dark ears and long hairs either side of the nose coming, and know that I've got to hide in the bottom and close my eyes. The small furry thing stirs my water and tries to draw me up to my roof. Sometimes I have to cling to the leafy thing on my floor with my tiny teeth to stay down. One time, she came in for a swim but didn't like it for her home. Her legs and body were splashing and flinging water all over the place; made a heck of a mess, until a sharp claw caught on some long material and she scrambled out, complaining with high-pitched squeals. She still visits, putting her face up to my big window, her eyes following me round and round; then she will open her mouth wide, show off her teeth, dip a foot into my water, flick it, then hop down.

Hot Rocks

I'm okay with her now. I know she likes me but doesn't really like my home.

The big furry thing likes me too. He thinks he should be my window cleaner but he is not very good. He sticks out this big pink thing from his mouth and licks, leaving wet trails of sticky bubbles with lots of little chunks of that muck that he eats mixed in. It has to be cleaned properly by the tall, not-furry fixit thing when the big furry one has gone.

Once the big furry thing pushed my window bubble to an edge where it almost balanced, then teetered and fell. I was flung out onto the floor where I struggled for breath. I wallowed from side to side. I gasped. I begged for water. The big furry thing bounced backwards and forwards over me making lots of excited noise. Luckily my tall, not-furry fixit thing came in, grabbed one of those portable soft window things, dipped it into my neighbour's temperature controlled place adding some water then scooped me up, most indecorously I felt, and dropped me in, then gently floated my new home on the neighbour's roof.

I sucked the water through my gills ... I can breathe again ... I'm alive.

The tall, not-furry fixit thing watched me closely with his big bulbous eyes framed in black, then returned my bubble home to the flat place it normally lives, replaced the leafy things, weighed them down with pebbles, filled it with water, then floated my new window on my roof, while he removed the water on the floor. When the tall not-furry fixit thing had finished, he poured me from the portable window back into my home.

My home ... my home. It was just as I remembered it. I relaxed and swam round and round.

Did I tell you I love swimming?

I love how with a flick of my tail I move forward, and with a double-flick go really fast.

Terror in the Outback

Diane Jensen

'Well, here we are Curley-Joe, the Tennant Creek pub. I believe buddy, this is our thirteenth pub stop over the four days since we left Sydney. What ya reckon mate?' Curley-Joe just eyed me. I started to explain to him I was only going in for a six-pack and bag of ice, but his attention was caught by – 'Oh my goodness look at that!' I exclaimed. Curley-Joe was rigid, sitting upright glaring out the window.

'Okay, boy settle,' I soothed. What we were both looking at was roughly half-a-dozen tray-back utes in varying degrees of disrepair, alongside us, outside the pub. Each one held a working dog on the tray. 'Whoops.' I quickly wound up the windows just in case he thought it might be fun to take them on. Open slather, being that Curley-Joe was a medium-sized domestic, mixed-breed pet.

I dived out of my trusty HR panel van and zipped into the pub. A few stares from the cowboys and others – well I'm used to that. They start from my blonde locks, travel over my bra-less tank top, then the short shorts, and I do have long legs, nicely tanned. Then they wander back up.

'Travellin' on yer own love?'

'No, I have a friend.' Well, Curley-Joe is my friend.

Hot Rocks

Returning, I threw the ice and beers onto the seat to sort out later and quickly pulled out. Further up the road, wound down the windows, put the ice and beers into the esky and we continued on. Curley-Joe was my borrowed companion for the return journey to Kununurra and he was a bit of an unknown quantity. His owner remained in Newcastle and would meet up with us when he also returned to Kununurra. So far, Curley-Joe had behaved perfectly. His only weird habit, which became quite endearing and funny, was his barking madly at every bridge we crossed, over creeks or rivers or culverts whether there was water in them or not. Cattle grids also got him going.

The temperature was rising as we drove. My old van had no air-conditioning and I reckoned it was about 35 degrees already. Up ahead was a sign pointing to some sort of man-made lake. We were only about forty-five minutes from Tennant Creek but I thought, why not? So we turned off and arrived at an oasis in the wide open hot country. No one there. Great. Curley-Joe jumped in first and I followed fully dressed. It was the coolest way to drive, in wet clothes. Ten minutes later, with an ice-cold beer in my hand, we drove on.

Reaching Four Ways Roadhouse, I topped up with fuel, bought a sandwich and we turned left towards the Territory. Curley-Joe enjoyed a Schmacko and a bit of the previous night's chicken, and settled down to being bored.

Hot Rocks

On we drove. Wide open, flat, hot country, occasionally scrubby, the odd tree here and there but nothing much else. I fell into a dream state as you do in country like this and drove on for a couple of hours. I'd been traversing the wide open spaces for years and loved it. Needing a bit of 'wake-up' I grabbed another beer and put a cassette into the slot. The last one got chewed up – the dust I think – so I hoped this one would play okay. It was fine and I rocked along. Hadn't seen another vehicle for hours, other than two huge very stinky, cattle trains that overtook me, so I wasn't really watching out for anyone. I only do 80 kph to conserve fuel and keep the old girl happy. Up ahead, on the left, was a billowing mass of dust. *Hmm. What's that?* I wondered. As we drew close, I saw a large herd of cattle being driven along the fence line by three fellas on horseback and a couple of dogs. Slowing down a little so I could watch them, and checking the rear view mirror, I was surprised to see a vehicle behind. It was very close behind me. Looked like a sedan. Pulling over onto the shoulder so they could pass easily, I realised it also slowed down. *What's the go here? Why don't they go around?* After having my fill of watching the cowboys as they expertly moved the cattle along, I signalled, pulled out and resumed my 80 kph speed. The sedan behind did the same. *Hmm.*

For dinner that night I'd planned to have a fire, as usual, and cook some beef and veg. in the camp oven. Curley-Joe would be ecstatic, as he knew when the camp oven was on his bowl would be full of the same yummy food. So I needed to stop earlier, pull off down some track away from the highway, collect wood and get the fire going, all well before dark. It was still stinking hot even with the sun settling down in the west. I grabbed a third beer, put yet another cassette into the slot. We rounded a slight bend and, checking behind, the sun hit the car still travelling at the back of me. I saw clearly there were three men in it. This was ridiculous. Putting my right blinker on to suggest they pass around me, in my head I urged that they do so. They didn't. I slowed down. So did they. I resumed a faster speed and the car stayed right on my tail. Sweat on my body from the day's heat suddenly turned cold. I didn't like this. They could have been following me for much longer than I realised, and from where? Could it have been Tennant Creek or Four Ways, or somewhere else? Following me, they definitely were.

'Curley-Joe,' I said, 'I think we have a problem.' He sensed my tension and became agitated, standing up, looking at me, flopping down on the seat, and repeating the moves. Fear was tightening my body. There was nothing and no-one in sight on the long road to the west and into the setting sun. By now, all thoughts of a campfire dinner were gone. I kept driving. They were still on my tail. Oh why were there no vehicles on the road I could flag down for help? So many thoughts flashed through my head and I began shaking. The sun was ready to sink and in the outback I knew it would become immediately dark – there was no 'in between'. *Keep going* was all I could think. The risk of kangaroos, emus, stray cattle could be no worse than this fear of what would happen if I stopped. Please God, I thought, there has to be a cattle station somewhere, but would I see one in the dark? By now, I was terrified and barely able to drive, shaking, sweat dribbling into my eyes. *I don't want this to happen! It can't happen!* The last of the sun's red-coloured rays disappeared and with a trembling hand I switched on my lights. So did they, the glare of their lights in my rear view mirror blinding me, stoking my fear of the evil behind me. *Something, please something save me, help me!* They were so close behind, right on my tail. I reached out a hand to Curley-Joe.

'You wouldn't survive out here mate, once they're done with me,' I told him, beginning to cry. He flopped down again and put his head on my lap. My heart was thumping so hard, I thought I'd burst. Suddenly I was tired, so very tired, the adrenaline flagging.

'No!' I screamed. 'Don't give in.' Reigniting my survival instinct, I turned off the cassette player, realising it had played over and over, and put my foot down, not caring about my speed. They were still on my tail! The road ahead was sloping to a rise and with all my heart and mind I prayed for a miracle on the other side. I couldn't go on much longer.

And there it was. To my great surprise, my headlights picked out a red telephone box. A telephone box? Way out here? But I couldn't stop to use it! They'd be onto me before I could get inside. *Oh my god*, just in time I spotted a track, through open gates alongside it!

I swung off the highway, showering stones and almost losing control. Tearing up the track, not daring to look if they were still behind me, I drove like a maniac. There were lights, a building, utes parked outside. Pulling up in a shower of dust and noise, I threw open the car door and jumped out screaming, just as some men rushed out of the building.

'Help me!' I shouted, and crumpled to the ground.

A couple of hours later, my ordeal over, my story told, I'd stopped shaking and these wonderful cowboys, with their cook fussing over me, fed both me and Curley-Joe. I was exhausted. Meanwhile, one of the men had grabbed a rifle, jumped into a ute and screamed off, back down the track. On his return later, he said that no car was found. He had driven some twenty kilometres to the west but sighted no-one.

'They could be anywhere out there,' he said. The men agreed I had to stay the night in the building which was their quarters and cookhouse. They were all so kind on the heels of my ordeal, that I kept tearing up. One drove up to the station manager's house to report the incident and see what could be done to find those monsters. After a welcome cool shower, I fell into a bed provided for me with Curley-Joe at my feet, safe at last. Before I could sleep though, I had one question to ask.

'Why the phone box at the station gates?'

'Well, one of the men said. The boss had it put in so we wouldn't all use the house phone to call family and friends! Also he thought it would be helpful for anyone broken down on the road, or for the truckies to use if they needed.'

'I want to thank him,' I said, tears pouring down my face. 'That phone box saved my life, because if it hadn't been there I would never have seen the gates and your track.'

'He'll be happy to know that,' another of them said. 'There's one thing more to do. Before you leave in the morning, we've decided to go out in two utes and drive both directions for a half hour or so and make sure those blokes are gone, as am I sure they will be, by then.'

With great relief, feeling safe and reassured, I fell into a deep and dreamless sleep.

Australia

Terry Dunkley

Allow me to sleep

Under a starry sky

Snug in my swag

The place is outback

Remote from the coast

Away off the track

Losing all cares

In the land of my dreams

Always to love Australia, it seems.

R.I.P

Craig Slobin

Bo was not overly worried, not yet. Johnny was just late, that was all. He was not answering her texts, but it didn't really matter. She'd played her part and he would play his. At least she had a torch, though with every passing hour the batteries were getting weaker and its light fading. No matter. She had what she really wanted in any case. In the dimming torchlight, the statuette of the Mother Mary in her other hand gleamed and glittered yellow. It was a solid gold piece, and the reason she was trapped inside this mammoth crypt. Well, not trapped, not really; her husband Johnny would let her out. It was his family tomb and his plan too, and a brilliant plan at that.

It had taken intelligence and bravery to do what they were doing without anybody the wiser. There were no witnesses to the theft. That was why Bo was stuck inside the crypt for the nonce. It was Johnnys plan for her to secrete herself inside his aunt's coffin, as she was interned in the tomb. A fantastic idea it was. Nobody would suspect she was in here stealing the family treasure. Bo was grateful old Auntie Melanie had finally died. The last family member had expired two years ago, so they'd had to wait that long to put their scheme into action. Nobody looked like dying again any time soon either. Bo was also grateful that Melanie was not too long dead. If she had begun to rot, Bo surely would have been dry-retching at the stench of death and would have given the game away as the coffin was put in here.

Now she waited. Johnny was going to open the crypt, using heartache for his aunt as the reason for wanting to gaze upon her one final time, with the priest as a witness to nothing being amiss. Because of the treasure in here, a priest was always present when the tomb was opened. Bo could sneak out behind their backs while they looked on poor Melanie. If either tried to steal the statuette with the priest here with them, it would be impossible. But not this way; this way Bo had plenty of time to waltz about in here with no one the wiser. It was unfortunate that the tomb could not be opened from the inside, else she would have freed herself hours ago.

Truthfully, she had almost tried to bolt out this afternoon when another relative was unexpectedly entombed. Whoever it was must have been distant blood, because she'd not heard of another funeral being planned before Johnny had secreted her away in Melanie's coffin. The family members at the impromptu funeral had been few, too few for her to get out without being noticed.

Her phone's beep indicated it was close to dead, so she quickly texted Johnny again to ask when he was coming. Still no response – and then the light on the screen went out.

Before making herself comfortable for the wait, and with her curiosity piqued as to the identity of the newly-dead relative, she decided to have a look. The coffin lid creaked as she lifted it; her torch blinked on and off with its very last energy.

And Bo's knees buckled as, filled with sudden terror, she found herself staring at Johnny's cold, dead face.

It Had to Be Brown

Christopher Hammond

The smell was beautiful: cinnamon, cumin, allspice, cocoa and others, all together in a heady mix. I remember knowing there was something not quite 'right' about the smell but it was so nice it *should* be right. At about this stage, awakened by the clashing of pots and pans, my mother came out of her room.

I was a bit over two years old and it was three in the morning. I'd left my bed in the dead of night to make a cake: my first cake. Not knowing anything about the art of baking, I relied on what I'd observed first hand: cakes were brown. I rummaged through the pantry and pulled out everything I could find that was brown and food-like. Every brownish herb, brown sugar, soy sauce, golden syrup, even vegemite made the grade.

Next I had to mix the cake. Mum had let me mix cakes before. It was about the best thing in the world, to be a part of making something so amazing, so I had a fairly robust grasp of what to do: throw everything in the bowl and stir. I stirred, gradually transforming the mixture into the worst cake imaginable.

Once my poor parents had woken up and come to witness my miracle, I insisted it be brought to life. The other thing you did with cakes was make them hard, in the oven. I needed to bake this cake. My mother tried to humour me: we'd bake it in the morning, she said. Let's just put it in the freezer for now. A bit reluctant, I eventually agreed.

I'm sure she hoped I'd forget once I'd had some sleep. But of course not – although she did manage to persuade me it was already 'cooked'. The freezing process had made it hard, which is what a cake needed: substance.

Unfortunately for my parents, I still expected them to eat the cake. I watched them closely as they pretended to eat my monstrosity, giving appreciative murmurs and telling me I'd managed to make a 'very nice' cake.

Then it was my turn to eat. I remember the disgusting taste well, more than thirty years later. It was, of course, impossible for me to admit my masterpiece was flawed, so I tried to convince my parents I thought it delicious. Naturally, they weren't so stupid as to believe me.

The cake was put back into the freezer for safekeeping until we would be hungry enough to eat more. It was never mentioned again.

Fire in My Veins

Denise Delaney

I was earth.
I was water.
I was air.

I was tree,
then I was fire.
Burning, crackling, popping,
spitting incandescent embers
onto the land's great hearth.

I glowed red, I glowed white.
I smoked.
Eruptions of grey
and raven clouds
jet-streaming,
circumnavigating the world,
creating fiery crimson sunsets
and red moons,
forming a thin circlet of soot,
falling slowly down.

I cooled.
My limbs brittle,
sucked dry
then charred.
Skeletons drawn black
against a rusty orange sky.

I am the germ of new life
embedded in roots of the old,
deep within the earth,
breathing,
waiting for water.

I will be tree.
Again.

FLASH FICTION

Flash Fiction is not for the faint-hearted.

Writers by nature can often be prolix and the challenge here is to limit the story to a shorter word length – 100 words or fewer, 300, 500, 1000 – all are acceptable as long as the stories comply with the general parameters of short stories.

Only a few of our members submitted stories for this section.

Faded Rose

Stella Perkins

She was last year's Valentine. I wallpapered the room with rose-flowered paper; rose-perfumed paper lined all the drawers. The garden was filled with new rose bushes and I looked at Rose and the world through rose-coloured glasses.

But now the climbing rose is crowding out my garden and I am weary of the cloying rose perfume. I long for something fresh, something minty clean.

The girl at the delicatessen always chews Minties. Her breath smells divine. She wears a mint-green-and-white-checked pinafore and ties her pigtails back with a smart green ribbon. I bought fresh minted potato salad there last week. Delicious.

A Rose's life is but a day. It fades and then ...

20/20 Hindsight

Denise Delaney

Young, sensuous.

Exploring her sexuality with temporary partners then becoming aggressively masculine in the pursuit of pleasure.

Faster.

Lower.

Harder.

Experienced, yet naïve enough to believe her potency could be proven by seducing a priest away from his godly mission.

Hmm ... it wasn't the challenge she was hoping for.

First Love

Denise Delaney

I remember those nights of delicious food and wine.

I showed you all of my hot spots, and you taught me to laugh and sing during sex.

You trained me, then you were gone.

I never had a man afterwards who wasn't personally offended by my trilling or my hilarity.

Census Collector

Diane Jensen

She sat straight-backed in a chair, hard against the wall. Her swollen, trunk-like legs led to feet planted together on the floor in fluffy pink slippers. Her face was ethereal and hardly lined. I learned she was eighty-nine years old. Her carer had just showered her and the walking frame was unobtrusively poked into a corner.

She smiled. It lit up her face.

'I always sit here in the morning sun,' she said, 'and as long as there is something to look at, I'm grateful to be alive.'

I handed her the Census form and explained the collection details. She said her daughter would help to fill it in.

I asked her what she enjoyed looking at most, because the area of her view was limited.

'Oh the clouds that change and form new shapes. The different birds with their amusing habits. The wind's influence on trees and shrubs, causing them to dance to their own music. I watch people too, wandering around, climbing in and out of cars, or standing about chatting. I often imagine what it is they talk about. Occasionally little lizards delight me with their darting around, and it's surprising how other insects play and cavort just to entertain me.'

I so admired her bravery and light. Her love and enjoyment of life for one so incapacitated left me awestruck and humble. It was hard to turn and leave her.

Fantasy Figure

Denise Delaney

Shiloa lies beside Philtriano, drifting in a post-coital funk, her languid eyes barely open, observing her man.

His is a satisfied pose, arms akimbo, splayed, everything about him from the La Gioconda smile to the soft, flaccid, tensionless muscles speaking 'replete'. In his dreams he relives the encounter, adding more erogenous zones to explore, a more cataclysmic orgasm, kundalini spiralling up and down his spine, then memories of extra arms and legs.

Shiloa moves. She changes. Buds appear on her torso in a helix pattern. They grow, they extend, they develop muscles, sinews, blood vessels, digits, then arms, pale skin with a fine cashmere fur in a ridge down the centre. Her body hardens, toughens, becomes more angular and a phallus erupts from her crotch.

She touches him and he begins to soften, becomes rounder, more sinuous. His penis disappears into his groin, his breasts enlarge, orifices appear. She strokes a line from his throat to his crotch. He groans, emerges from his stupor, and utters a sigh. She leans over him.

'This time Philtriano, I'll be the man.'

Pain In The Neck

Craig Slobin

Twang! ... Crack!

There goes Jonny. Kind of fitting he should go first, after all, he was the first to fire his musket. Hell, he already had it loaded and ready to go. None of us others had. No doubt hell was where Jonny would end up too.

As for the rest of us, well, it was probably a 50/50 thing. Old Gussy would make it to heaven, or at least to the Pearly Gates. He was a devout man, pious even; aside from this business, of course.

Twang! ... Crack!

Goodbye Teddy. Now, Tedwin there was a good man, too. I doubt Jesus and God will take that into consideration, however. He was a good man until you pissed him off, once riled up he would kill you as soon as look at you. No, angry Teddy will be feeling Lucifer's flames for all eternity just like Jonny will. Once again, it's only fitting, I suppose.

Henry had been the fool to plan it and the rest of us had been even more foolish by agreeing to it. Yep, pompous Henry was the ringleader and deadly Jonny, angry Teddy, old Gussy and myself his stooges. Was it worth it? Probably; of course, it would have been worth it a lot more if we hadn't been beaten. Not beaten up, though that did happen. Even my own mammy wouldn't recognise my face after the pummelling I received when we reached dry dock.

At least with my face so swollen and bruised, dear sweet mammy won't realise I'm up here if she's somewhere in the mob howling at us. Or what's left of us.

Twang! ... Crack!

See you in hell, Henry. Hmmm, I wonder if there's women in hell? I hope so. It's because of women we're all here as a matter of fact, or the lack of women on the supply ship. Who could blame us for wanting to jump ship in Tahiti? All of those half-naked, copper-skinned beauties on the beach were the true reason we tried to mutiny. After eight months at sea even the ugly, fat ones were pleasant to behold.

What are you smiling at, Gus? I may as well give you a wink for the trip.

I smile back. 'See you later, Gussy.'

'Not bloody likely, Tom,' he says. 'Not where you're going, matey.'

Well, that's nice, isn't it?

Twang! ... Crack!

Ha! Not smiling now, are you, Gussy?

Crikey, this drizzle is freezing my bones. I wish I didn't have to go last. At least hell is warm, I might even enjoy it. As long as I don't have to listen to Henry and Jonny's bitching for eternity.

'Hood?' asks the executioner.

'Nah,' I reply, I may as well give him a wink too. Not his fault, it's just his job, isn't it? 'Just make sure the noose is tight, matey.'

Twang! . . . Crack!

Crocodile

Denise Delaney

'Mum. I don't like crocodiles. They're big and slimy and have rotten dead-fish breath. They have rip-you-apart teeth and they hide in rivers and billabongs where they eat people.'

'This crocodile does not ever eat people.'

'But he will. It's in the crocodiles' handbook of things they must do. They sneak underwater, grab people by the legs, and roll them round and round 'til they are dead, and then they stash the body in tree roots and eat them little bit by little bit whenever they get the hungries and when they get caught they cry huge fake tears.'

'Oh, young William. He's not that kind of murderous crocodile. He's gentle and loves to play in pools.'

'Why is the crocodile at my party? He doesn't eat mud cake, or lime jelly, or fairy bread or fruit salad with ice-cream, and he has nothing to say unless we are playing the 'repeat after me' game. I want him to go away. Shoo croc. Get lost. Go, go.'

His mother clasps his shoulders. 'Billy, You're are being very foolish. Settle down.'

He shakes her off and winds himself up. His face becomes red, then burgundy, deep maroon, and finally 'glow in the dark' purple. He kicks the table, which shudders and wobbles then stabilises. He boots a chair that falls backwards, lands with a thump, shakes, then is still. He screams, 'Make him go away!' grabs a fork and stabs, piercing the crocodile's skin.

With a delicate sigh, the crocodile slowly loses its air, settling into a pile of plastic, creased and folded in awkward angles over a small, square metal box that repeats endlessly: 'Help, he hates me. Help, he hates me. Help he hates me.'

I Bled

Stella Perkins

I woke up with blood all over the sheets.

I cried to my Mother.

'You are now a woman,' said she.

'I do not want to be a woman. I do not like all this stuff to catch the blood. I want to be a child again. I feel like I have died.'

'There is no going back,' they said. 'You are a woman now.'

There was no going back but I had lost something precious and I felt dead.

'Come,' he said, 'I'll make you a woman.'

And he smiled and took my arm.

Into a dark and lonely place he led me and took off my clothes one by one until I stood naked in front of him.

'Come,' he said. 'I'll make you a woman.'

'No!' I cried.

He stole something precious.

I bled.

But so did he.

Then they found his bludgeoned bloody body.

Finally I felt like a woman.

The judge concurred.

'I'LL BET SHE LIKED THAT'

We asked our writers to begin their stories for this
section with the above phrase, which was
chosen at random from a novel at one of our meetings.
Writers found unique and inventive ways to weave
stories – both fiction and non-fiction – around this
phrase.

Puccini

Barbara Harvey

'I'll bet she liked that,' said Mary.

'Well, no, she didn't,' I said. 'She was furious.'

'But why? I don't understand.' We were Christmas shopping and exchanging stories of our childhoods. So I told Mary about that disastrous Christmas.

'Every Christmas, Mum complained she only received impersonal gifts: a cookery book or a new iron, things like that. So, this year Dad decided to buy her something personal and asked me to help him. I was about ten years old and didn't really know what things Mum liked; she wasn't easy to buy for. However, I was thrilled Dad asked me to go as I didn't get to spend much time with him.

'We were pretty broke in those days. Dad worked as a long-distance truck driver, away from home for four to five days at a time. Mum had a low-paid part-time job. Our parents' relationship wasn't great and tensions were strained when Dad was home. It didn't take much for Mum to let fly. Most of their earnings were spent on essentials with little left over for luxuries, but throughout the year, Mum saved money into a Christmas fund so she could get something nice for us, as well as put a decent spread on the table.

Preparations started early: fruit cake made at the end of October and stored in an airtight container until marzipan and royal icing were added at the end of November. A week later came the iced decoration. I was allowed to help and there was a real build-up to the Big Day. My brother and I grew more and more excited as it drew near. We always had friends visit on Boxing Day when we played games and cards until very late into the night. We so looked forward to this happy time.

'Dad and I couldn't decide what to get. We looked at lingerie and clothing, some toiletries I felt Mum would like, but nothing appealed to him. Then Dad went into a music shop and looked through the records. He saw a boxed LP recording of *Madame Butterfly* and said it would be perfect as he remembered Mum saying she liked the music. He'd bought a second-hand record player earlier in the year but had forgotten she'd complained about it, saying he'd wasted money as it wasn't a necessity. I suppose I should have said something then but he seemed so pleased with it, I didn't want to spoil his pleasure.

'We left the shop with the gift and I was sworn to secrecy. Mum kept asking me what Dad was giving her but I didn't let on. However, on Christmas morning, when she tore off the wrapping, she certainly didn't react as we'd expected.

'"Why have you given me this!?" she demanded.

'"Well, you said you liked the music," replied Dad.

'"Only the song 'One Fine Day'," she snapped back. "I've never heard the complete opera. There are so many other things I need – a twinset or stockings – things I can't afford to buy for myself! You'll have to take it back. I hope you kept the receipt."

'And with that Mum grabbed all the torn wrapping paper and empty boxes and disappeared to the kitchen. She berated me later for not telling her, but I hadn't wanted to be disloyal to either Mum or Dad. As I often did, I felt pulled in opposite directions by the two of them. Feeling miserable, I disappeared to my room to be alone.' I gave a wry laugh. 'Things settled down for Boxing Day but it was very frosty between Mum and Dad until he went away again. It was a Christmas I'll not forget.'

Barbie Bike

Christopher Hammond

'I'll bet she liked that,' said my mother. I was on the phone, telling her how the nurses at Westmead had presented my friend Sarah's daughter with a Barbie Bike, complete with training wheels, when she left the hospital. She'd been there for a very painful three weeks, during which her femur had been replaced.

I rolled my eyes. 'Think about it, Mum,' I said, 'What would Lotus do with a bike?'

'Oh my god, you're right! What on earth were they thinking?' Eleven year-old Lotus had Type 2 OI, also known as Brittle Bone Disease. Even slight stumbles could result in serious bone fractures.

'I dunno,' I said. 'I'm just driving up to Armidale with Arianwen to see them now. I'll let you know all about it.'

When I arrived, Sarah had carried her daughter inside to her bedroom, where she would spend most of the next few months healing from her surgery and manoeuvring her full leg cast with a great deal of difficulty. I found them both perched on Lotus's bed, staring at the bike, which was sitting there resplendent in pink, complete with coloured streamers.

'Why the hell did they give me that bike, Mum?'
Lotus asked. 'Christo, do you think I *should* try riding
it?'

Sarah and I were was just as mystified as Lotus.
Sarah shook her head. 'Well, even though it's got
trainer wheels you could still fall off and hurt yourself
pretty badly. But it's your choice, darling. I haven't got
a clue what they were thinking when they gave you
that. I suppose it was nice of them, but.'

'I just don't get why they gave it to me. I'm gonna
be in bed for months; even after that, I could fall off
and hit my head or something, or hurt my back. Can
the doctors put metal in my back? Like, in my spine?'

'No, mate. You could wear a helmet but they're
kinda crappy.'

'How about if I cover myself with bubble wrap and
sponges?'

We laughed. 'Yeah,' said Sarah. Probably your only
hope.'

'Well bugger that then. How about we give it to
Arianwen? She's almost six and she's just about big
enough to ride it. I'll bet she'd like that.'

Arianwen being my daughter, I knew she'd be
thrilled. 'That's very sweet of you, Lotus,' I said.

'She's not getting my Barbies, though,' warned
Lotus. 'In fact, I can hear her out there on the deck

playing with them. Tell her to stop, and can you put them back in my room?'

'But you don't play with them anymore,' protested Sarah, a little embarrassed, while I went to do as she asked.

'That's not the point. She can have the bike though. I don't want that thing. It's way too dangerous.' Lotus continued to stare at the bicycle. 'What did they think I'd do with it?' she wondered.

Arianwen, of course, was thrilled and duly grateful.

'Good riddance,' said Lotus, as she watched me pack the bike in my car. Then she looked wistful. 'Even though, it might have been cool to ride a bike.' She turned away and switched on her Nintendo.

Poor Lotus, I thought. *The only excitement she'll be getting for the next few months will be virtual.*

The Nine to Five Grind

Craig Slobin

'I'll be bet she liked that!' laughed Hender, as he ducked a spear thrust, stabbed forward and punctured the enemy warrior's liver.

'No!' answered Ander with a grunt as he kicked into a man's chest, hurtling the bearded man backward. 'She didn't!' He leapt forward and plunged his broadsword into him.

Hender chuckled before he called out again, 'Ware! Left!'

Ander bent at the waist and his offsider rolled across his back, slicing a new enemy's neck as he landed on the other side of him.

'What'd she say!?' Hender asked in a shout to be heard above the din of battle on the rocky beach.

'Ware! Left!' Ander hollered back. Hender squatted down and Ander leapfrogged him sideways to the left. He had no time to stab the man with the round shield, so smashed his face in with the hilt.

'Well?' demanded Hender while gutting a younger, clean-shaven enemy; perhaps he was too young to grow a beard. 'What in the hells did she say?' Ander grimaced as three big men confronted them.

'Two me, one you!' shouted Hender. Ander presumed he should take the one on the left as he was on that side now.

They both grunted with the exertion of slashing out with their heavy swords. At least Ander still had a shield, not that Hender needed one; his longsword was a foot longer than Ander's and he used it like an axe lopping timber, except this timber was muscle, sinew and bone.

His friend howled with laughter as he felled their legs from under them. Ander only just beat his man. Hender was so much quicker, even against two, that he had time to bend down and retrieve one of the enemy shields.

They both somersaulted over the sharp rocks and used their powerful legs to propel themselves erect again. Rowing a boat for hundreds of miles every summer enlarged all of their muscles: arms *and* legs. When they stood upon their feet again, they roared with adrenalin and slew the next two fools who confronted them.

'She said I can't come a viking anymore!' shouted Ander. Hender grinned through his blond beard, spun in a three-sixty, and cleaved a man's head clean off. The blood splattered everywhere and Ander frowned at his friend as he quickly wiped gore off his own beard.

'Be more careful, you bastard!' he cursed. 'I hate the taste of blood!'

Hender ignored him as he slid down between the thick legs of a large man. The giant went down with a cut to his groin and Ander was there to yank his offsider to his feet as the enemy came on.

'What are you going to do!?' shouted Hender.

'We made a deal!' he yelled back. 'My wife will let me come a viking . . . as long as I don't bring any more Saxon women home!'

They both erupted into laughter as they charged up the beach.

A Christmas Tale

Denise Delaney

'I'll bet she liked that.'

'I'll bet she hated it.'

'Mum's always loved a bit of extra money at Christmas. She always whingeing about the cost, and the numbers of relatives and hangers-on arriving empty-handed.'

'Yeah. But Dad's in the doghouse for a month when he gets back from the races.'

'Just put your money where your mouth is.'

'Okay. Ten bucks it is then.'

After a traditional, gut-stretching lunch, the oldies are off for a 'nanna nap' while the rest of us head to the shade of the camphor laurel tree and settle, with eskies and food for our 'picnic races'.

We pull straws with the winner determining the 'race' and we've had some beauties.

We've bet on how quickly the rising creek would burst its banks (two hours thirty-five minutes, just long enough to help get the animals to high ground).

The most scandalous bet was when Aunt Lola arrived, (preceded by the rumour that she was a he) wearing a bustier, one of those stretchy, strapless top things, and proceeded to get drunk and raunchy and I picked her as good for seven minutes before a boob would swing up and over and stay out. A second bet on how long it would take her to notice, came in at three minutes nine seconds, and would have gone longer but Uncle Bob went goggle-eyed staring.

Two years past it was blisteringly, stinking hot, so hot that even the flies refused to take to the air, although they did a mean 'Aussie Crawl'. In a 'why not' moment, we decided to break-test the thermometer in full sunlight. We watched it climb, with cousin Ben doing the race call.

'We've reached 45, 45 and rising, 48, 49, 50, there's no stopping it today. 60, 65, 68.'

At 72 degrees Ben lost his momentum and lay down to have a short kip.

At 103 degrees, helped along by a magnifying glass, the thermometer broke, dripping mercury in tiny, silver balls onto the crunchy, dry grass. Uncle Bob threw his arms in the air and tried unsuccessfully to assume the winner's pose. He was a bit under the weather, our Uncle Bob.

Last year during the drought we counted the ants that invaded our picnic blanket converting our sweet treats into their movable feast. With accusations of double counting, and demands to 'put your bloody glasses on', we couldn't reach an agreed number. No winner declared. We decided Mum, who hated gambling with a passion, should have the takings and I made a bet she liked that. She didn't but she took all the money anyway.

It's too dusty for the usual cricket match, and the enthusiasm for gambling seems to have gone, so we all, dogs and cats included, shift inside to airconditioned comfort where we drape ourselves over chairs and lounges, a sprawling, untidy menagerie, with arms crossed over our bulging bellies.

Another family Christmas out on the farm.

Unwanted Memories

Desley Polmear

I'll bet she liked that. Molly read the last line to her sleeping granddaughter, Kate. She closed the book and watched the little one's chest rise and fall, then pulled the covers up over her slight body and placed her favourite book on the bedside table. She sat for a while in thought, wondering about Kate's future. 'Precious little darling,' she whispered, kissing her on the forehead. Molly poured hot water into the teapot, secured the lid and put the china cup on the tray. She carried the tray to the study, setting it down by the computer. She had been writing her life story for over a year now but recent events had altered her life's path.

Kate had just turned three when her mother Leanne was taken away to prison, after being convicted of the murder of her husband Craig. Kate would be a teenager by the time her mother was freed. Molly had tried to warn her daughter of Craig's outbursts of rage. She saw it early on when they were dating but Leanne knew best. Her daughter hid the abuse, cancelling appointments, keeping Kate from childcare. Molly had feared for both their lives many a time and she feared one day one of them would be found dead. Drugs or alcohol were not involved; he had a short fuse. Her daughter walked on eggshells most of her married life.

'Mum ... help me? I've killed him!' Leanne yelled down the line one day in the heat of summer. 'What'll I do? Mum, please, help me?' Molly remembered the painful cry of her daughter and the continuous screaming from Kate. No mother wants to hear the distraught pain in her child's voice. It will stick with her until she takes her last breath. Molly herself had grown up with her father's abuse of her mother. She believed now that her dead mother was finally at peace. Her father lost two women the day her mother died because Molly never spoke another word to him.

Although Leanne hired a well-known and successful lawyer, she was still sentenced to fifteen years. If she behaved, she'd be out on bail after ten. Molly reckoned the law had no empathy for her daughter's years of suffering at the hands of a monster. She saved the file, closed down the computer and trudged off to bed.

'I didn't think you'd ever get here,' Brian said. Molly smiled. Married for thirty-one years and she still loved him as much as ever. 'I'm ready for a nightcap,' he said, spooning into her.

Giggling, she turned towards him. 'I know what nightcap you want,' she said, pulling the string loose on his pyjama pants.

When she heard his soft, even breathing, her thoughts went to Leanne, locked away in the cold prison cell. As always, she prayed for her safety.

Breaking Security!

Diane Jensen

'I'll bet she liked that!' Ashley hooted down the phone.

'She loved it. As usual with our Jules, if rules can be broken to get what she wants then she's onto it. Sure, the Security chased us out in the morning, but what a laugh! We spent the whole night in the men's quarters, had food from the canteen, partied with free booze and a bed to sleep in. Jules of course stayed with Chook – a farewell bonk on our way out of town.'

'But how did you get in?' Ash asked.

'Jules got the goods from Chook. We went onto the third track past the mine, gate open, and in we sailed, 'I said. 'Gotta go Ash, Jules wants a pee and it's my turn to drive.'

I took the wheel and we hit the highway; not a vehicle in sight along the black tar, flanked by miles of red dirt, occasional brilliant-coloured rocky hillocks and the odd emu, as we headed south on an escape road trip from Kununurra.

'We just wanna be free, oh yea, free oh yea!' we belted out at the tops of our lungs. Jules zipped off the ring pull from the first of our icy-cold six packs sitting safely between us. Laughing and slurping our beers with the hot desert wind blowing through my trusty HR panel van, we agreed that Argyle Diamond Mine would be tightening up their security.

'We're on the road again!' was the next song the wind tore from our mouths. Doing 120 ks in the outback no problem, and no police to pull us over.

Weeks later, when we returned to Kununurra, it wasn't long before friends and workmates showed us the story in the local rag about two women who'd broken security and got into the Argyle Diamond Mine.

'Where do you reckon we'll camp tonight, Dizzy?'

'Jules, remember, don't call me Dizzy in company, okay? But I think if we top up our big esky with ice for the beer at Fitzroy Crossing, and we've got sausages, then the cliff top over Ninety Mile Beach would be a great camp.'

'That's a plan,' she replied. We flew down the highway, dodged a stray bull, slugged two six packs and pulled into Fitzroy Crossing pub, stirring up the red dirt and debris.

'Never paid this much for bloody ice before,' I grumbled as we roared out of there, escaping the locals and their requests for smokes and beer.

The wind roared around us on the clifftop, rocking the wagon. It was dark and eerie. We cooked the sausages on the bed in back of the panel van, while we lay on each side of the pan, which splattered on the gas cooker. The swag would remain on the roof.

'Never done this before,' Jules laughed, as we scoffed down cheap wine. Our beer, of course, was for day travel.

'Mate, this is going to be a "never done this before" road trip all the way to Perth,' I said, laughing.

Brand New Car

Lucy Powter

'I'll bet she liked that!' said neighbour Steve to Darryl, as lots of people came to offer their congratulations and shake his hand. It was such a magic night. I stood beside Darryl, grinning with joy. The look on my face was enough to answer Steve.

Darryl and I had moved to Canberra. We had joined the local club which was holding a new promotion to run over six months ending just before Christmas. The prize was a brand new, shiny red Toyota Corolla sedan. It looked beautiful as it sat in the foyer of the club.

As the months rolled by, members talked about it and admired it, opening the doors and boot. I fell in love with it at first sight and at every opportunity sat in it, just to smell that aroma that permeates a new car. I used to dream about it. We had never owned a brand new car. Over the many years of our marriage, our cars had always been second-hand, being all we could afford. Like many people, we had a mortgage as well as the cost of putting our youngest son through four years of university.

This promotion was the first big one the club had undertaken. Members entering were handed tickets which were put into a barrel. Then each month, tickets were drawn and these were kept for the final night. A core of 120 members turned up on the Night of the Draw. On that night a further draw was conducted and as each member was called that person went on stage where the manager was holding a bag containing 120 keys. As they chose their keys they would try them in a huge padlock which sat on a small table facing the crowd. Only one could open it and the person turning it would thus win the car.

There was much excitement and noise in the club and everyone who held a ticket was hoping they would win. We had arrived with a group of friends. Each of us had about three or four tickets in this draw and we were all hopeful.

Many people held their breath as each person walked onto the stage, chose a key and tried the lock. An audible sigh went up as the lock held. The anxiety and excitement was palpable as each unsuccessful member sat down.

Then, Darryl's name was called. So, followed by lots of good wishes from our friends, while I held my breath, he put his hand into the bag and pulled out a key. The key turned in the padlock and in the hush, a loud click was heard as the lock sprang open.

A cheer started, soft at first, then building up to a loud crescendo. I screamed with excitement and happiness and jumped around like a kid. Darryl's beaming face told the story. We had won the car!

We were wined and dined by the management and invited to pick up the car the next day. We were the proud owners of a lovely, shiny red sedan, straight from the showroom.

A Grievous Insult

Margaret Drury

'I'll bet she liked that,' guffawed the oafish Rodney, his voice coarse.

I was furious. He'd discovered through some drunken old cronies at the pub that my mother, as a young woman, had been much admired and sought-after in our village. He was daring to imply she was a loose woman. I had never liked him and even though he was supposed to be my husband's friend, I told him to get out. He leered at me and groped my bottom, so I slapped his face – hard.

I knew he'd had a few drinks but that was no excuse for such rudeness. Just wait till my husband got home! He was on an overseas trip and not due back for another three days. Rodney had taken it on himself to be my guardian. *Horrible old creep*, I muttered to myself as I showed him the door and told him not to return until he was sober and prepared to apologise for the insult to my mother.

What I didn't realise, was that my seventeen-year-old son Jack was just outside the room, overhearing the exchange of words and the insult to his beloved grandmother. As Rodney went out the door, Jack grabbed him by the collar and the inebriated Rodney was in no state to resist. Before he knew what was happening, Jack had dragged him off to the bathroom and shoved his head in the toilet, flushing the water twice.

'That'll teach you to insult my grandmother,' said Jack as he pushed the gasping, dripping Rodney out the door. 'I don't think my dad will want you around anymore, so sling your hook!'

Rodney staggered away down the footpath and, to my relief, that was the last we ever saw of him.

Up in Smoke

Robin Hammond

'I'll bet she liked that!' I said, waving neighbour Frank inside. I'd been running the best cocaine outlet in Nambucca and Frank had bought up big for his sister's 50th. Belinda, my luscious trophy wife, had a little sideline, giftwrapping the drugs for special occasions: ribbons, bows, tiny bits of silver stuff. They looked real good when she'd finished. Frank said his wife got a kick out of it.

Anyway, this particular morning I was off to the bottle shop when Frank arrived for some more of the good stuff. I let him in and stepped outside, checking the cellar door was bolted. Only Belinda and me knew about our crystal meth lab and I was keeping it that way. Had a coupla bikies down there, wrapping and parcelling, ready to set off up the coast with a stash of ice.

So – walked off, feeling good about things. Never thought, back in the 70s, it would come to this when I started growing pot. Lived in Byron at the time with me first wife, Sylvie. We were pretty hard up. I'd lost me job at the council and Sylvie's work as a salesgirl didn't bring much. In fact, we was having trouble paying the rent, when I had the idea of growing marijuana on the

229

patch of bushland next door. Big success it was, and we was sitting pretty for a coupla years until we come home one arvo to find the cops all over the place, running sniffer dogs up and down the yard. We hit the gas and kept going south.

Eventually landed on a commune outside Bellingen, where we reinvented ourselves; dropped acid, smoked weed and changed our names. I was Hemlock. I grew dreadlocks, wrapped meself in a loincloth and lay around scheming. Sylvie became Phoenix and wore ankle-bells and feathers in her earlobes. Then she hooked up with a scrawny hippy, big brass ring through his nose. I was a bit pissed-off but, by then, hydroponics had become the thing. Without too much effort on my part, I was soon loaded again.

That's when I decided on Nambucca, and not by mistake. Locals call it 'Mt Druitt by the Sea'. Perfect. Built meself a luxury home, acquired the trophy wife, changed me name to Neil. Invested in real estate as a cover then built a state-of-the-art meth lab. Got the idea from *Breaking Bad*. Thought it was the best idea ever; I was raking it in. Had a team of bikies running stuff up the coast and even a few golden oldies carrying it interstate in their caravans – supplementing their pensions, they said.

Just musing away like this, halfway to the bottleo, I hear an almighty fucken explosion and up goes the house, along with the trophy wife, the two trophy kids, neighbour Frank, two bikies and Charlie, our labradoodle!

Well, they'd told me the stuff was unstable and it seemed they was right.

Everything come to an end with that godawful bang and now here's me in the Mid-North Coast Correctional Centre, awaiting trial. Don't know what I'll get; lawyer says it'll be big. All those bodies make the difference apparently. People seem to be most upset about the bloody dog – weird, eh?

Fuck, it was great, though. Yeah, I miss the kids and all that, but I been busy scheming again. Reckon once I get to know the guys I'll get a racket going. Have a nice little nest egg ready for when I get out if I play me cards right. What could go wrong? Life is what you make it, as the saying goes.

Undercover

Stella Perkins

'I'll bet she liked that!'

'You should have heard her blow her stack. I couldn't believe a woman could swear like that.'

'Oh, she's been around, believe you me. She spent a period of time on the wharves undercover, dealing with the drug crowd that thrives in that kind of environment.'

'I have no idea what the boss wants her to do now.'

'No. It was a strange thing, to pull her out in the middle of an operation. Do you know what's going on?'

'She always keeps her cards close to her chest.'

'That's about the only thing that is close to her chest. She has a rare asset in those boobs.'

'Yeah. Pillow talk is the ideal way to get that extra titbit of information, and that is no pun.'

'Here's the boss now. He'll give us the facts.'

Enter the Boss with the woman in question.

'What's the big idea Boss?' she storms at him. 'I was just gaining ground; another minute and I would have had him eating out of my lap.'

'Precisely. However, I have a job of world-shattering importance for you now. A serious threat has been made on the life of the American President. Your job is to see that it succeeds.'

Bon Appetit

Terry Dunkley

I'll bet she liked that, thought Claude as Janine finished his carefully-prepared meal. They had met in the office several weeks ago and become attracted to each other: he for Janine's good looks and she for his intriguing French accent. For the past six weeks, Claude had been trying to persuade her to let him prepare a true taste of French cuisine at his flat.

Eventually, Janine accepted the offer. 'But,' said Janine, 'no snails. I can't even bear the thought of such things. Or oysters; I don't have the stomach for them. So revolting!'

'Of course, ma cherie, no escargots and no oysters – it is a good thing you tell me.'

Claude had picked her up in his battered old Citroen and driven her to his flat. The perfect gentleman, he had quickly run to her side of the car to open the door and held her hand as she alighted.

Janine was quite surprised at his flat. It was very cosy and had a scented candle burning – such a nice touch. Claude was obviously out to impress and it was working. Janine was feeling very comfortable.

'Please sit here,' said Claude, 'and I will get us an aperitif.' He went into the kitchen and returned with two tall glasses, a half bottle of Pernod and a bottle of Perrier spring water from the fridge. He poured a little Pernod into each glass and then topped them up with spring water. Janine watched, fascinated, as the clear Pernod, when mixed with the clear water, became cloudy, and when she sipped, the aniseed taste reminded her of her grandmother's favourite seed cake.

They went to the dining table, where Claude served a seafood bisque in the French Mediterranean style but, true to his word, minus the oysters. It was exquisite and tasty, and followed by a lemon sorbet to neutralise the palate. Then the main course was served with a bottle of Beaujolais, elegantly presented and consumed with delight.

'So, ma cherie, did you enjoy your meal?' asked Claude, removing her plate.

'Oh yes,' said Janine. 'It was absolutely perfect. And the quail was delicious.'

'Quail!' exclaimed Claude in horror. 'I would not give you quail ma cherie; I give you only ze best. It was ze legs of ze frog!'

FIVE WORDS

At each of our meetings we set homework to be written before the following fortnight's session. Usually it takes the form of what we call the 'five words' homework.

We call out five random words and the task is to write a story of up to around 500 words that contains those chosen five somewhere within it.

The challenge is to ensure the words – and it is ideal they be completely mismatched – fit seamlessly into the story. Sometimes, for an added bit of fun, we choose five words beginning with the same letter, as with the first selection of stories following, in which the chosen words all begin with 'P'.

In the following examples, we have included at least two stories in each five-word category to show how disparate our stories always are.

Words: perpendicular; pop-top; parrot; pompous; passionfruit.

Prickly Pop

Denise Delaney

One last Passionfruit Headbanger and all inhibitions fly away. This man is gorgeous. He leans forward and gently licks the side of her face, nibbles her earlobes and softly whispers, promising her silky skin sliding on his muscled torso, the double-backed beast on overtime, much joy, and his willingness to take her to heaven and back.

She is standing perpendicular to the floor, his hands resting lightly on her waist when her knees buckle and she slides down. His hands catch on her elastic top, which rolls, dragging her breasts up, then stops caught at her armpits, leaving her bosom pointing to her shoulders. With a shudder and a shake, they drop down, fully exposed. *Damn*, she thinks, *my stretchy top has morphed into a pop-top.* She sighs, then relaxes to the sensation of his hands and tongue exploring her erogenous zones.

***

Two years later, she visits her father at the big house, her toddler clutching her hand. She tries to hug her father but he frowns, pulls away and puts out his hand.

'Penelope my dear. Taking up child-minding now?'

A voice in the background says: 'Child-minding now! Child-minding now!'

'I have been Daffodil-Rainbow for years, Dad, and this is my son, your only grandson. We named him Passionfruit, to honour his conception.'

'His conception! His conception!'

She ruffles her child's orange hair and leans down to kiss him.

'Still playing the hippy, Pen. What are you after now? And with your bastard child in tow. You shamed me and now you wish to rejoin my family?'

'My family! My family!'

'Dad, you are as pompous and as small-minded as ever. Still five-foot-six and eight foot up yourself. I hoped you had changed.' She stalks off, muttering under her breath, 'Bastard!'

'Bastard! Bastard!'

Her father clenches his fists then yells at the parrot: 'Shut up, you feathered little shit-for-brains.'

'Shit-for-brains! Shit-for-brains!'

He goes to a desk, takes out a pistol, checks it is loaded, aims at the parrot and fires. *Bang!* Feathers flutter up in a small rainbow-coloured cloud, then slowly float down.

'Bang! Awk ... awk ... aw...'.

The parrot topples to the ground, making a tiny thud, and never speaks again.

Words: perpendicular; pop-top; parrot; pompous; passionfruit.

Pressure Pot

Diane Jensen

Joey's poptop caravan lay idle out the front of his purple-painted house.

'Hey Joey,' his obnoxious neighbour piped up. 'When are you going to piss off that heap of shit? The neighbour always spoke with such pomposity it got Joey's back up. He gritted his teeth and ignored the man.

'Well?' said his neighbour, Colonel Pisspot-Pank. Joey was trying to enjoy a bit of private meditation, horizontal on the soft clover patch under his peppercorn tree. Percy, his favourite pet parrot, was artfully parading up and down on Joey's chest. Percy made little p-p sounds as he moved over Joey's chest, which calmed Joey and helped promote his meditation. His neighbour was a piffling nuisance.

It happened that Colonel Pisspot-Panks's wife Pearl, was inside Joey's house making a pot of tea. They'd just enjoyed a passionate session of love-making and Joey idly hoped she would stay there until the Colonel left. He didn't really care.

'Not very productive are you Joey?'

There he goes again, Joey sighed to himself. 'Pressures of life, Colonel, pressures of life,' he said, still remaining prone.

The pompous Colonel padded closer and propped his ugly great person against the peppercorn tree. He eyed Joey's paddleboard and paddle, standing perpendicular against the tree.

'Oh please, Joey, what pressure are you under?' he sneered. Joey, fed up with this prick, eased himself up and waved in the general direction of the poptop.

'In answer to your first question, you see that passionfruit vine over there?'

'You mean the one that's perpetuating its growth over your disgusting poptop?'

'Yes,' said Joey. 'The purpose of my leaving my poptop there is to provide a nice prop for my passionfruit vine to grow over. And in answer to your second question regarding the pressures in my life – well, after the last profoundly orgasmic love-making session today with your wife Pearl, she proposed to divorce you and move in with me! A particularly preposterous idea, I told her. So you see Colonel, the pressure is on me. Anyway, right now, she's pottering in my kitchen making peppermint tea. Would you like to partake of a cup?'

Words: perpendicular; pop-top; parrot; pompous; passionfruit.

Pretentious Parrot

Christopher Hammond

My wife has a pet parrot and I'm afraid it's stealing her away from me. In the mornings, she feeds it passionfruit from a spoon at the breakfast table. My cornflakes taste like chalk as I watch it nuzzle her flagrantly. I can't believe the pomposity of the damned bird; its airs and graces drive me mad.

'I'm going out to the van,' I say.

My wife barely notices me leave. I stomp out to the pop-top in the backyard. Running perpendicular to the roof is my new parrot death trap. I'll make my move soon, when my wife leaves for yoga. By the time she gets back, it'll be killed and plucked and waiting in the oven.

It will be an ex-parrot.

Words: draconian; selfish; treachery; baleful; pathway.

Backseat Driver

Robin Hammond

I married a backseat driver. If I'd known, I would never have married him. After all, I am the daughter of two driving instructors and thought I'd escaped the horrors all that entails, when I finally left home.

There were early signs, I admit. For instance, Stanley had a set of draconian procedures to be adhered to before we went to bed. Every room in our house had to be cleaned from top to bottom. We dusted, vacuumed and polished into the small hours. As soon as dinner was finished, we began the cleaning. If I put the spice jars back with their names facing anywhere but out, he would direct a baleful glare at me and straighten them until their labels were in perfect line. There were other rules I had to follow, to keep peace in our house. It is all too tedious to relate, so I will spare you the details, but believe me when I say draconian is putting it mildly.

Neither of us had a car, so when my parents offered me one of theirs, because they were upgrading to a later model, I grabbed it. I suggested to Stanley we should drive around Australia, picking up jobs along the way. I did not tell him I thought this might be the pathway to a more adventurous and carefree life.

I could not have been more wrong. Being a born-and-bred city man, Stanley had never learned to drive but he thought he knew all about it anyway. Our car, having been used to teach driving, had dual controls. This enabled Stanley to stamp on the brake or clutch whenever he so fancied – which was often.

In Tully, we collided with a cane tram. I saw it too late and accelerated. Stanley figured I wouldn't make it and stamped on the brake. The tram only nicked us but we were shaken up. Nevertheless, it didn't stop Stanley. In the Top End, we were charged by a water buffalo – same thing happened. This time, the radiator burst. Water poured out and we were stuck in a tropical downpour that quickly turned the road into a bog. The whole thing was hellish.

We continued through Western Australia, South Australia and Victoria, jerking and swerving all over the place, until we came to an isolated spot in Tasmania. Around a bend, I hit some gravel. I knew how to drive out of a skid and was in the midst of doing so when Stanley grabbed the wheel *and* stamped on the brake. Over the precipice we went, rolling onto a ledge, landing upside down. I remember watching our roll of toilet paper unravelling all the way down the mountainside.

Climbing out, we perched on the narrow ledge, waiting for a rescuer – no mobile phones in those days. We waited a long time. Finally, a ute driven by one of the flannel-shirted locals rounded the bend and stopped. We'd been arguing for some while and were sitting back-to-back. The driver climbed out, surveyed us and the trail of toilet paper – this caused him to smirk a little – then offered a lift for some help; he only had room for one.

Stanley was not selfish; he suggested I go, and I leapt at the chance. I retrieved my handbag and it was only when the driver eventually dropped me off that I made a snap decision. A bus waited at a nearby store; the destination sign said 'Devonport'. I paid the driver, jumped aboard and was off in a jiffy.

Later, when I was aboard the ferry chugging across the Bass Strait, I realised my actions could have been considered treachery. I pictured Stanley perched on that ledge as the cold night set in. He'd have to crawl back into the car for shelter. I was pretty sure nobody else would come along at that time of day. Maybe his movements during the night would rock the car off the ledge. It was a long way down.

I smiled to myself as I snuggled into my cosy bunk, lulled to sleep by the waves.

Words: draconian; selfish; treachery; baleful; pathway.

Haunted

Diane Jensen

The opening paragraph of her thesis read:

> Young girls pregnant with illegitimate babies during the 1950s to 1970s were treated by professionals in a draconian manner. They were made to feel ashamed, and usually were. They were told they were on the pathway to hell. They were selfish, careless, and no better than whores. Treachery and lies smothered them in their vulnerable and pitiful lives, up to and including the birthing of their babies. They were unable to have an opinion or choice about any procedures. Questions asked about the changes in their bodies, the birth procedure and aftermath, were treated with disdain, and usually remained unanswered. These girls had no 'rights', often being told so. Social workers also had a negative impact on these girls, along with the nurses, sisters, matrons, doctors. To even consider keeping their babies was met with explosive derision. They were 'not worthy'. They were forced into girls' homes or sent into families and treated like slaves. They were not allowed

```
to gaze at the faces of the babies
they had given birth to. Not even
for a brief moment. Their babies
were whipped away, never to be seen
by them.
```

Sarah stared balefully at her written words. At this point in her thesis, she probably should cite some of the sad and miserable interviews undertaken with women willing to tell how it was. She shuddered and felt sick. She continued typing from her notes:

```
Many fell under the banner of
mental illness. Some committed
suicide. Some of them never got
over it. Some of them searched
faces in the street, in cafes, and
on public transport. They searched
for years, trying to imagine what
their children might look like as
they grew older: always haunted.
```

'Why have I chosen this subject?' she moaned. But she knew why, and hit the computer keys again.

Sarah had lived it, and would never forget. Somewhere out there was her beautiful baby.

Words: draconian; selfish; treachery; baleful; pathway.

The Switch

Christopher Hammond

I'd been living under the draconian rule of my mother for eighteen years now, and I was finally leaving.

'Well, I'll be glad to see the back of you, you selfish girl,' she said to me at the breakfast table. She was shovelling eggs into her mouth and regarding me with her small, piggish eyes; I knew she blamed me for my father's treachery, she'd told me often enough.

'He was a monster, doing that to me,' she said, this morning. A regular tirade was beginning. 'It's the treachery of all men, not just your father. You must beware. The men of the world, they'll chew you up and spit you out, girl. You mustn't be like them.'

'Yes, mother. Please excuse me, I need the bathroom.'

I left the table, making sure to curtsy in the doorway. I could feel her baleful gaze following me. I hurried to the bathroom quickly as I dared, stepping lightly, locking the door behind me. I listened. Silence. Hurriedly, I raised my hated skirts and urinated standing up, very loudly. If my mother caught me doing this I'd be punished, but I took the chance, luxuriating in my betrayal. Years ago, she'd threatened to cut it off if she ever caught me weeing like the boy I really was. I knew she'd do it, too.

My suitcases were packed and a taxi was booked. I gathered my scant belongings then, finally, the secret present from my father, a wrapped parcel that was dangerous to own.

I waited at the front step for the taxi. Then my mother appeared. I couldn't help but stare at the bag my present was in. I hoped she wouldn't notice, but she was beyond caring. She cannoned into me, weeping.

'Don't leave me, girl,' she said. 'I'll be alone without you. I'll die alone.' She was crying heavily now; she'd never behaved like this before.

The taxi was coming up the driveway. I disentangled myself. 'I'm sorry, Mother. I'll be back to visit. I promise.' I gathered my skirts and ran down the pathway to the taxi. The driver packed my few bags away and I got into the backseat. As the taxi pulled away from my now-wailing mother, I was about to enact my own treachery.

I feverishly tore open my secret package. It was a suit: three-piece, houndstooth, silk bow-tie and gold cufflinks! I ripped at my dress, ignoring the taxi driver's exclamation: 'What the fuck are ya doing?' and soon I was clothed in my new outfit.

It felt strange and constricting and liberating. My father was waiting at the end of the ride for me. I was finally starting my new life – as a man.

Words: stupid; laughter; plaster; eggplant; hallucination.

Moussaka

Stella Perkins

'It is just a purple patch,' Ivy told herself. 'This feeling of doom can't last forever. Soon it will pass, the birds will sing again and the flowers will show their colours.' But the fog seemed to swirl all around her and everything appeared cold and grey. She pulled her dressing gown tighter and moved away from the window towards her bed.

Through the thin plaster wall, Ivy could hear their post-coital laughter. She had listened earlier to their panting and carrying-on. It was all too much. She was being stupid. People were entitled to joy, lust and happiness. Just because she had been rejected once, did not mean she would always be alone.

Time for action. She slipped into her UGG boots and went downstairs to her purple kitchen. She would cook, get creative and make a moussaka. That would cheer her up. She assembled the ingredients on the black bench top: lamb mince, onions, garlic, celery, tomatoes, a jar of béarnaise sauce, parsley and the glossy purple eggplant.

Ivy sliced the onions and garlic and, while their fried fragrance filled the kitchen, she raised the knife and viciously stabbed the tomatoes on the chopping block. The juice splashed onto the black-and-white tiled floor. It made her laugh and she stuck the knife into the firm, purple eggplant. The pleasure she felt as the knife sliced effortlessly through! It could have been – it should have been – right through his leather jacket. But no, it was just an hallucination.

Ivy's feet slid on the tomato juice. She felt herself slither slowly down to land on the kitchen floor. The knife cut through her leg and her blood mixed with the tomato juice, forming a red pool on the black-and-white floor. Her last thought before she passed out was:

There is a message here for me, but I don't know what it is.

Words: stupid; laughter; plaster; eggplant; hallucination.

Hitman

Robin Hammond

Dearest Charlene:

I have a confession to make. I am a CIA Hitman.

Yes, you've been married to me for forty years and, like everyone else, believe me to be an upstanding pillar of the community, a benefactor to the poor and disenfranchised of South West Rocks. And it is true. Together, we funded the new Medical Centre; we built the bridge across the river to Stuart's Point; and, in my role as de-facto mayor of the Rocks, I established the 20-storey casino on the Horseshoe Bay waterfront, a very popular undertaking. And that distinguished-looking plaster statue of me on the clifftop overlooking Little Bay, the one that won Sculpture in the Gaol last year: I know you love sitting on that bench overlooking the little beach and gazing at that statue. What further testament to propriety could a person have? So I understand you might come out with a bit of incredulous laughter at my claim to be a hitman.

When, in future, you think about what I have told you and find yourself veering towards disbelief, just remember that time when you awoke in the night and saw me framed in the doorway of the ensuite, cocking the safety catch on my pistols. That was a slip-up on my part, I know. But at least, then, I was able to persuade you it was an hallucination brought about by all the LSD you'd been using.

I'm not stupid: I've been able to build and maintain a water-tight cover. I will admit to feeling guilt over the many lies I've had to tell you, my darling. Twenty years ago, when we came to the Rocks, I fully intended to retire. But my reputation followed me and I've had to do the odd job from time-to-time. Have you never wondered why we are so wealthy, even though I've never actually appeared to *work* at anything? Whacking people is pretty lucrative, you know, especially when the job entails somebody very important.

Which brings me to why I'm writing you this difficult confession. Yesterday, my CIA superiors spoke to me on Skype about a very grave matter. They have ordered me to assassinate a Soviet spy, whose identity they have recently discovered. She has eluded them for many years and, although she has not been operative for the last twenty of those years, the pride of the United States makes it essential that, now she has been revealed, she must be eliminated. Tonight they emailed her name to me. To my great shock, I discovered it is you, my dear Charlene!! How have you managed to deceive me, your husband, for all these years? No matter. I am telling you all this because I'm giving you the chance to disappear before the deadline (no pun intended). So flee, my darling, as fast as your legs will carry you. I know your Soviet minders will have a safe house for you somewhere, maybe even in the United States itself! What irony that would be. Perhaps, one day, I will defect so that we can reunite.

All my love forever dearest.

James

p.s. One thing I will really miss is your delectable eggplant dip. Would you mind leaving behind the recipe when you go?

Words: synergy; apricot; voluminous; designs; harpsichord.

Madame Louvier

Lucy Powter

Madame Marguerite Louvier, the owner of House of Marguerite, arrived in her chauffeur-driven car at the front door of the huge warehouse-like couturiers' salon. She was curious to know why Veronique had called her the previous evening, leaving her a cryptic message on her answering machine. Her leading fashion designer greeted her and ushered her through to her office where a tray was set up with coffee and biscuits and Eloise, their newest model, stood wearing a voluminous, multicoloured dress.

'This is called a Kaftan and it is one of our new designs for the coming season.' Veronique gestured excitedly. 'There is nothing like this coming from the other salons. We believe our kaftans will target a wider age market.' Marguerite walked over to Eloise and examined the kaftan, feeling and pulling the material this way and that, letting it glide through her fingers like a multicoloured waterfall, catching the sunlight streaming in the large window.

'It is magnifique!' exclaimed Marguerite, straightening up. 'You have indeed the right support, cooperation and synergy in the workshop to achieve such goals. Will you be ready for the fashion parade in a few weeks' time?'

'Yes,' said Veronique. 'We have all supplies, materials and seamstresses at the ready, and the models are available. Did you want to see the Grand Salon since it has been painted in the apricot and white colours you requested?'

'Yes,' replied Marguerite as she followed Veronique out of the office. 'I also want to talk to you about the music for our parade. I have contacted Monsieur Armand, our musical director, who suggested 'Summertime, Summertime' by the Jamies, a hit in 1958 and in 1962. Since the harpsichord is the only instrument on that song, he agreed to play it at the parade for our models to walk to.'

'Sounds perfect,' agreed Veronique. 'I think everything is taken care of now, Madame.'

Words: synergy; apricot; voluminous; designs; harpsichord.

Discord

Diane Jensen

As his fingers flew over the keys, the old fella's head suddenly dropped onto the harpsichord. The audience gasped. The instrument produced loud, discordant notes and then died.

Alarm rippled through the onlookers.

A woman in voluminous skirts broke through and darted to him. Her gown of apricot with geometric designs, swirled between the legs of the harpsichord stand as she first reached for his wrist, checking the pulse, and then his neck. She sank to her knees then looked up, shaking her head.

'He is gone,' she said, and began to weep.

People shuffled, looked around. Some moved off and others expressed their shock, not knowing where to look or what to do.

'Who is he, what's his name?' someone called.

The woman, still weeping, straightened up and asked for someone to call for an ambulance.

'Does anyone know his name or where he lives?' a voice rang out.

'He's my father,' the woman said, attempting to stem the flow of her tears. At that, more people with saddened faces moved off; after all what could they do? The man who had last called out, stepped forward, holding the hand of a young girl.

'Can I help please?' he enquired. 'Your father, you said. You must be very proud, he was a wonderful musician. The synergy of his music was amazing. My daughter and I often stopped by to listen to him. The way his fingers just flew over those keys mesmerised me.'

The woman nodded, sobbing. 'He was very famous once,' she managed to say, 'but his life went wrong. I will miss him.'

The ambulance arrived, and he was gently lifted onto their stretcher and into the ambulance. They obtained details from the woman, whose name the man learned was Sylvie, and drove off.

'I'll help you with the instrument,' he offered.

The man's daughter, who by now had become restless, tugged at her father's jacket with wide, questioning eyes.

'Yes, I know Katy, but we'll talk about it later. We must help this lady first.' Sylvie guided them to her car. She reverently packed in the harpsichord and turned to thank the man. He introduced himself as Jeremy Jackson and his daughter Katy who was eight years old.

'I used to be a policeman but I took early retirement because of an incident which involved my daughter that, sadly, caused her to stop speaking. So you see I have some experience of tragedy.' He gazed fondly down on Katy.

'You ... you, you're the one,' Sylvie stuttered, with a horrified look. She took a step back glaring at him.

Jeremy was shocked at this sudden angry outburst. 'What do you mean?' he asked. Then a look of recognition spread across his face.

'You put my father behind bars! You helped sentence him for a crime he didn't commit! He didn't touch your little girl five years ago. It was someone else!' she shouted at him. 'That's why he was finally acquitted. That's why he lost his career in the Russian orchestra!'

Sylvie gathered her skirts and threw herself into the car. She accelerated into the traffic, speeding away.

Words: grateful; lively; acrobatic; pansies; exposition.

Also use the following sentence somewhere in the story: He stood alone on the veranda, his eyes wet with tears.

Ponytail

Robin Hammond

She shook off his restraining hand, ran along the path and climbed aboard the motor bike, throwing her arms around the leather-jacketed waist of its rider.

Kevin peered fretfully through the gloom as his ponytailed daughter disappeared down the driveway in a spray of gravel and an earsplitting roar from twin exhausts. He should be grateful, he supposed. At least Pamela hadn't run away from home like some of her friends. Sharon, for instance, had been locked in her room for attending a rock'n'roll concert against her parents' wishes. In an amazing acrobatic manoeuvre, Sharon had climbed out her window, edged along the guttering by her fingertips, swung into a tree and climbed down, disappearing into the night. But, unlike Pamela, Sharon had always been a lively young lady and such behaviour was almost to be expected of her.

But what to do about his precious daughter and the company *she* was keeping? He stood alone on the veranda, his eyes wet with tears. There was no doubt about it, he had to admit the terrible truth: his daughter had turned into a widgie.

Those young hooligans she was hanging around with. What did they call them now? Bodgies, that was it, with their leather jackets and their dreadful oily, ducktail hairdos. And now boys wearing pink shirts! *Pansies*, the lot of them. Keven patted his *very* short short-back-and-sides, and tucked in his crisply-ironed white cotton shirt. Bodgies and widgies – and his daughter was one of them, decked out in those tight pedal pushers and swinging that damned ponytail everywhere she went. Only the other day she'd been sent home from school for refusing to take it down.

When the war ended, he'd thought all his troubles had gone with it. Pamela, their bundle of joy, had been presented to him by his young wife Nancy, who then died two days later. They all said he couldn't bring her up by himself but he proved them wrong. True, she wasn't the boy he'd hoped for but he'd got around that by dressing her in dungarees for a while and teaching her the delights of a Meccano set. Later, he'd take her on his arm to the opera, making sure she had a good classical music education.

It seemed all that had been for nought. Only yesterday, he'd come home to find her *jiving* in the living room while she watched that awful Johnny O'Keefe screaming about being a wild one, or some such rubbish. *And* she was smoking his Craven As. Teenagers, they called them now; as though they were a different breed or something.

He thought hard, long into the night. Next morning, after delivering the usual exposition to Pamela about her errant ways, while she chewed gum and effected an air of boredom, he headed for the hardware shop. He bought chains, ropes, bars for the tiny cellar window and padlocks for the cellar door, together with a camp bed, gaslight and small chipboard table. He knew what they'd all say when Pamela disappeared. She'd have run away to join her friend Sharon, wherever *she* was, and he wasn't going to disillusion them. He'd set up a tape machine and play non-stop opera, day and night, into that cellar, via a loudspeaker through the window bars. He'd been a prisoner-of-war and knew something about brainwashing.

He picked up the garden shears. First thing, though, he'd chop off that ponytail as soon as she stepped through the door. She'd soon come to her senses; he knew she would.

Words: grateful; lively; acrobatic; pansies; exposition.

Also use the following sentence somewhere in the story: He stood alone on the veranda, his eyes wet with tears.

Optimistic Acrobat

Diane Jensen

Carla had hoodwinked him again! Big-time! Reg was feeling murderous.

'Bloody woman! How could I have let this happen!?' Smokey looked up, puzzled, and back-stepped at his master's outburst, his bum hitting the screen door. Reg glared, then softened. He flopped down in despair. 'Sorry boy, not your fault, come here.' Reg fondled his ears, staring into the distance. His gaze dropped back to Smokey. 'I'm so grateful to have you mate. She's such a bloody bitch ya know.' Smokey rubbed his head against Reg's hand in doggy consolation. 'You'd never ... aahhh!'

Reg clutched his chest, sliding to the floor as blackness enveloped him. *That damn pain...!*

* * *

Carla flitted about, gathering up the expensive, beautiful antique pieces packing them into storage boxes. *So what if some belonged to Reg? The old fool. I've got it all now.* She glanced, smiling, at the bulging briefcase by the door. It was identical to Reg's. She then moved to the bedroom, threw open the lid of the embossed leather suitcase and piled in her glamorous, top-of-the-range clothing.

Reflecting on the amazing, very bountiful, success of the exposition, she stopped to drain a glass of Moët. Reg was a useless wimp in bed, she mused, but he sure knew how to organise a successful show. And then, his agreeing to transfer all profits to a joint account from which they could quickly withdraw cash! Of course, she had done just that.

'Fly to the Gold Coast, change names, build a mansion, settle down together and live like royalty.' *His grand plans. No thanks, you old fart. I'm off far away. You and the cops will never find me! Would love to see your face when you open your briefcase full of nappies – you'll need them soon enough!* Carla laughed, as she remembered how easily she had swapped the briefcases.

'Gotta get lively now,' she said to the room. 'Time is of the essence.' Her plane was leaving in two hours. Soon, the storage company would collect the boxes and one day she would reclaim them. Meanwhile – the world awaited her. She was beautiful, clever and an expert manipulator. *Reg is just an amateur crook! He had his chance the last time I gypped him. Didn't get him for much then, and he came back for more!* Carla was glad to be rid of him and his devoted, slobbering dog she'd pretended to like.

* * *

Reg awoke. Bright light dazzled him. He closed his eyes. Recollections surfaced of doctors, pain and attached wires. How long have I been here? A hand gently shook his shoulder.

'You're one hell of a lucky man Reg. If it wasn't for that big dog of yours somehow dragging you from your house, you wouldn't be here now. We've given you a pacemaker. You had a bad heart attack.' Reg closed his eyes again as he remembered the nightmare of that day. The 'exposition day'.

* * *

Two weeks later, released from hospital, he looked over his flower garden, abloom with vibrant pansies. Smokey, his heroic companion, chewed on his reward: a big, juicy piece of beef. Reg clasped a newspaper, his shock at one article having nearly thrown him off-balance. It read:

```
The body of former acrobatic circus
performer, Carla Zammon, missing for
12 years from her famous circus
family, has been found amongst the
wreckage of Flight CN382, recently
shot down by a missile over the
Caribbean. Carla's family is said to
be griefstricken at the confirmation
of her death. Her whereabouts during
```

the years of her disappearance are unknown.

He stood alone on the veranda, his eyes wet with tears. They fell in admiration of his wonderful dog, but also for Carla, and all that money – gone!

CONTRIBUTORS

Denise Delaney

Denise read the household encyclopaedias and dictionaries as a child. She loved the accumulation of words, of facts and of ideas. This hasn't changed but, one day, fiction walked in through an open door in her mind and has been comfortably living there amongst the detritis of her other obsession – art – ever since. Denise writes poetry and short stories, sometimes illustrating them with delightful sketches. In her 'spare time' she creates colourful works of art, jewellery and pottery.

Margaret Drury

Born on New Year's Eve 1933, Margaret has always had a love of books, fostered by an aunt who regularly sent her a good book for Christmas, and a couple of teachers at grammar school. While bringing up her six children, there was not the time for writing. Now she and her husband are in residential care and she can at last have a go.

Terry Dunkley

Terry is a retired seafarer with a love of short story fiction writing. He draws characters from people whom he has encountered in his life. Sometimes there is poetic justice in his tales and invariably a refreshing twist to the finish. He has been published in the group's first anthology, *Tales from the Rocks*. He has a vast range of stories and some poetry to his credit.

Christopher Hammond

Christo is a new member of the SWR Writers Group and describes himself as 'undoubtedly their finest writer'. Along with his unbridled modesty, he is handsome, funny, smart and utterly charming. At 37 years of age, he's also extremely unpublished and he just can't wrap his head around why. Maybe it's something to do with the procrastination, for which he's infamous.

Robin Hammond

Robin has been a lifelong reader of literary fiction and non-fiction. She is a professional freelance editor and proofreader, working on books ranging from domestic violence to fantasy and many other genres. She has travelled and lived in Australia and Papua New Guinea and worked for many years at the University of New England in Armidale. Her books have been published by Australian publishing houses and in several overseas countries. Her stories and poems have appeared in anthologies and she has won prizes for her poetry and non-fiction. One day, she intends to write a book about her gangster uncle from the 1920s but is presently enjoying developing her skills in fiction writing.

Barbara Harvey

Reading and writing essays were not enjoyable subjects at school for Barbara; her imagination did not run wild with interesting stories. On leaving school, she entered the secretarial field, married and reared two boys. Her creative talents lay more in music and sewing. However, as the years passed, reading also became a bigger part of her life, her preference being for novels, especially those series that included an historical element. Recently retiring and moving to the mid-north coast, Barbara heard about the SWR Writers Group while attending another function and became intrigued. As her imagination has grown, she has occasionally thought there could be a story inside her and so decided to join the group to test this idea.

Diane Jensen

Devouring books from infancy influenced Diane's love of writing from school age, later in the form of letters to friends and family. She compiled these from nomadic wanderings throughout Australia and overseas, flavoured with some fiction. Her diverse careers, jobs and adventures have influenced Diane's writing. The SWR Writers Group is her current supportive and inspiring force to continue writing. Diane also writes poetry.

Stella Perkins

Stella has always loved writing but placed it on hold until her children left home and she joined the SWR Writers Group. Stella has taught in preschools, primary and secondary schools, TAFE, adult education, drug and alcohol rehabilitation centres, and in the prison system. She has gathered many stories from experiences during her four-score years of living. Her stories have been published in magazines and anthologies and she has published a book which is an historical fiction based on the story of her maternal grandparents. She also likes to write Flash Fiction.

Desley Polmear

Desley joined the SWR Writers Group in March 2008. From a young age, Desley often had her nose in books, like *Girls Own Annual* or those by Enid Blyton. Her other love was writing. Her teachers noted she had a great imagination. Her years of counselling gave her insight into other people's lives and helped her create stories and characters when writing her novels. Desley listens and observes at all times as she travels the world. Apart from her latest trilogy, she has published two other books. She is now busy writing about a murder in a tiny seaside village.

Lucy Powter

For most of her years, Lucy has been occupied by a nursing career and family life. On retiring, she and her husband left Canberra and travelled the east coast of Australia, choosing to settle in South West Rocks. An avid reader, she joined the writers group, writing short stories, many from her imagination and others from her life experiences.

Craig Slobin

Craig is a writer of fantasy and science fiction with a love of the unexpected twist, just like his life: from living in a Muslim country to being a crocodile hunter. His characters grow and evolve. But don't get too attached to them, because some may very well die. No matter the genre, his tales will be an emotional roller coaster. Since his teenage years, he has been engaged in writing a number of fantasy novels, yet to be published

www.ingramcontent.com/pod-product-compliance
Lightning Source LLC
Chambersburg PA
CBHW070446030726
47503CB00004B/911